Aunt Dimity and the Heart of Gold

Aunt Dimity and the Heart of Gold

NANCY ATHERTON

VIKING

VIKING
An imprint of Penguin Random House LLC
penguinrandomhouse.com

Copyright © 2019 by Nancy T. Atherton

Library of Congress Cataloging-in-Publication Data

Names: Atherton, Nancy, author.
Title: Aunt Dimity and the heart of gold / Nancy Atherton.
Description: New York : Viking, [2019] | Series: Aunt Dimity |
Identifiers: LCCN 2019005293 (print) | LCCN 2019006512 (ebook) |
ISBN 9780525522690 (ebook) | ISBN 9780525522683 (hardcover)
Subjects: | GSAFD: Mystery fiction
Classification: LCC PS3551.T426 (ebook) | LCC PS3551.T426 A93314 2019 (print) |
DDC 813/.54—dc23
LC record available at https://lccn.loc.gov/2019005293

Printed in the United States of America
1   3   5   7   9   10   8   6   4   2

BOOK DESIGN BY LUCIA BERNARD

For my readers, and their hearts of gold

Aunt Dimity and the
Heart of Gold

One

Christmas was coming and the weather was appalling. The pristine counterpane of snow that should have blanketed my little corner of the English countryside was nowhere to be seen. Dense fog infused with a ceaseless grizzly drizzle had turned my winter wonderland into a murky, mucky mess.

Although my husband, Bill, and I were Americans, as were our twin sons and our baby daughter, we lived in the Cotswolds, a pastoral haven described in countless guidebooks as one of the prettiest regions in England. Bill ran the European branch of his family's venerable Boston law firm from an office in the nearby village of Finch; ten-year-old Will and Rob attended Morningside School in the bustling market town of Upper Deeping; and I juggled the ever-changing roles of wife, mother, friend, neighbor, gossipmonger par excellence, and community volunteer.

Our daughter, Bess, who would turn two in February, was busier than the rest of us combined. She had walking down pat, but running was still a risky proposition, and her vocabulary, while growing by leaps and bounds, wasn't expanding fast enough to satisfy her need for self-expression. Her dogged attempts to keep up with her big brothers and to communicate with her doltish parents led to occasional meltdowns that sent our sleek black cat, Stanley, running for cover. On the bright side, the vast amount of energy

Bess expended during the day allowed her to sleep like a lamb at night. Every cloud . . .

I saw no silver lining in the shroud of fog that enveloped our honey-colored stone cottage. Having endured the vagaries of English weather for more than a decade, I knew better than to expect blue skies and bright sunshine at Christmastime, but the extended run of gray December days was beginning to get me down.

My late mother would have called it rheumatism weather, and I knew exactly what she meant. The frigid dampness seemed to creep into every joint in my body, creating aches and pains I associated with senior citizenship. An old bullet wound in my left shoulder made its presence known by throbbing intermittently, but my physical discomfort was as nothing compared with the mental dejection brought on by ten sunless days in a row.

I wasn't the only one feeling the effects of the rotten weather. Though the rain hadn't fallen hard enough to trigger floods in our river valley, it had put a definite damper on the festive season in Finch. A gray veil of mist clung to the picturesque buildings that bordered the village green, obscuring the twinkling lights and the glittering baubles that should have brightened our long winter nights.

To make matters worse, more than half of the villagers had been laid low by head colds or chest colds or head-and-chest colds, and though no one was at death's door, the afflicted felt as if they were. The rest found it increasingly difficult to exude Christmas cheer while scraping mud from their boots and wiping cold droplets of fog from their ruddy faces.

The Yuletide Blight, as my husband had dubbed the outbreak of upper-respiratory infections in Finch, had hit families in outlying farms as well. A scant handful of farmers straggled into the village each evening to enjoy a comforting pint at Peacock's pub, but those who came seeking respite from farmhouses filled with runny-nosed offspring were doomed to disappointment. Christine and Dick Peacock, the pub's hospitable proprietors, were distinctly under par. Their red noses, rheumy eyes, and hacking coughs made the pub feel homey, but not in a good way.

Peggy Taxman, the imperious tyrant who, with her meek husband, Jasper, ran the post office, the greengrocer's shop, and Taxman's Emporium, Finch's grandly named general store, and who, without Jasper's aid, chaired every community meeting in Finch, had been struck down by a crippling case of laryngitis. Since Peggy used her stentorian voice to intimidate anyone who dared to challenge her authority, her affliction had sent an unseemly ripple of mirth through the village, but it had also resulted in canceled meetings, reduced hours at the Emporium, and delayed deliveries of Christmas cards.

The tearoom's owner, Sally Cook, wasn't faring much better. Her husband, Henry, had ordered her to stay in bed after a prolonged sneezing fit had contaminated a batch of gingerbread men, two dozen freshly frosted Christmas bonbons, and a towering ziggurat of miniature mince pies.

Bree Pym, the young New Zealander who'd inherited a house near Finch, had gamely volunteered to wait tables and to manage the cash register while Henry took Sally's place in the kitchen, but with so many villagers down for the count, Henry didn't need Bree's help. He was more than capable of handling the trickle of customers who dragged themselves into the tearoom to purchase a box of uncontaminated Christmas treats.

The Handmaidens—my husband's pet name for the quartet of middle-aged women who'd once harbored hopes of riding off into the sunset with my well-mannered and well-heeled father-in-law—were the Blight's latest victims. By isolating Elspeth Binney, Opal Taylor, Millicent Scroggins, and Selena Buxton in their separate cottages, the virus had made it impossible for them to pursue their favorite pastime: meeting at the tearoom to share a pot of tea, a plate of scones, and a heaping helping of gossip.

Unfortunately, gossip, too, had taken a turn for the worse. In happier times, the village grapevine thrummed with all manner of local news. Hairstyles, clothing choices, ongoing feuds, upcoming events, behavioral quirks, and questionable horticultural decisions were just a few of the topics that would be discussed and dissected for days—sometimes for months—on end.

Ever since the Yuletide Blight had barreled into town, however, the only topic my neighbors and I discussed was . . . the Yuletide Blight. Who had a cold? Who didn't have a cold? How bad were the colds? How long would the colds last? Did old-fashioned cough syrups work, or should the sick put their faith in modern nostrums? Miranda Morrow, Finch's freckle-faced witch and a notable herbal healer, espoused natural remedies, but their efficacy was called into question when she, too, succumbed to the Blight.

A few lucky villagers had escaped Finch before the virus arrived. Old Mrs. Craven's good-hearted sister-in-law had swept her off to the South of France for the holidays, and George Wetherhead, the bashful model-train enthusiast who lived in the old schoolmaster's house, had gone to Brighton to attend a convention of model-train enthusiasts. When a timely telephone call alerted

George to the dismal state of affairs in the village, he wisely accepted an invitation to spend Christmas with a fellow enthusiast who lived well beyond sneezing distance of Finch.

To my great relief, the nasty bug hadn't yet infected my genteel father-in-law, William Willis, Sr., or Amelia, the splendid widow he'd married after spending much of his adult life as a widower. The happy couple lived up the lane from us in Fairworth House, the gracious Georgian mansion Willis, Sr., had purchased in order to be near his grandchildren after his retirement from the family firm.

With the coming of the Yuletide Blight, Amelia had taken the precaution of imposing a strict isolation policy on Fairworth House. Until the virus had run its course, she would allow no one—not even family members—to pass through the wrought-iron gates that guarded the entrance to the Fairworth estate. I couldn't fault her for barring the door to visitors. Will, Rob, and Bess missed their grandfather almost as much as he missed them, but as human petri dishes, they were potentially hazardous to his somewhat fragile health.

So far, the potential hazard had not been realized. For reasons surpassing my understanding, my brood hadn't fallen ill. Although Bill and I were on high alert for the slightest hint of a sniffle, we detected nothing. In the midst of so much misery, we were almost ashamed to admit that our cottage appeared to be a virus-free zone. When our neighbors brought up the subject, which they did, often, we found ourselves apologizing for our conspicuous lack of ill health. We felt as if we were letting the side down.

The vicar and his wife had also been spared, but the Nativity play had not. For the first time in living memory, an event that brought the whole village together had been canceled due to the limited number of villagers who could participate onstage, backstage, or in the audience without coughing their lungs up.

Since church attendance was at an all-time low, the Reverend Theodore Bunting had cut services at St. George's Church to a bare minimum in order to concentrate on home visits. While he ministered to the spiritual needs of his stricken parishioners, his wife, Lilian, who was of a more practical turn of mind, tidied their cottages, changed their bed linens, and made sure that their bills were paid on time.

Lilian and the vicar were ably assisted in their good works by the few villagers who weren't beset by illness. Mr. Barlow, the retired car mechanic who served as the church sexton as well as the village handyman, bustled from cottage to cottage, repairing furnaces, sealing leaky windows, and chopping firewood. Charles Bellingham and Grant Tavistock, who ran an art appraisal and restoration business from their home in Finch, went from door to door in the village, delivering gallons of homemade soup to the afflicted.

After Henry Cook declined her offer of help, Bree Pym became an errand girl, retrieving mail, purchasing groceries, and generally making herself useful to her ailing neighbors. James and Felicity Hobson, the retired schoolteachers who lived in Ivy Cottage, brought the bedridden armfuls of books and magazines, which they gladly read aloud upon request.

As the mother of a toddler whose immune system was still a work in progress, I was exempt from house calls, but I contributed my mite by decorating St. George's. It took ten times longer than usual because Bess insisted on helping me, but I eventually managed to set up the old-fashioned crèche, tie red ribbons to the pews, hang evergreen swags on the altar, arrange Christmas roses in the font, place sprigs of holly on the deep window embrasures, and decorate the stout fir tree Bill had erected beside the pulpit. While I worked I hoped and prayed that *all* of my neighbors would be well enough by Christmas Day to discuss and dissect my handiwork with their customary zeal.

My horse-mad sons spent most of their waking hours at Anscombe Manor, where my best friend, Emma Harris, lived and where she ran a well-respected riding school. Under her tutelage, the twins had become such accomplished equestrians that we'd had to stash most of their blue ribbons in a cedar chest. They were avid cricketers as well, but not even the thrill of a well-bowled googly could compare to the exhilaration they felt while galloping over hill and dale on their beloved gray ponies, Thunder and Storm.

Sadly, the foul weather had derailed their plans to spend Christmas break in the saddle. Emma couldn't in good conscience allow her star pupils to gallop through dense fog over slick hills and muddy dales, but they didn't rail against her restrictions. As true horsemen, Will and Rob were content to clean tack, muck out stalls, fill hayracks, tend water troughs, groom horses, and exercise them in the indoor arena all day long. They would have slept in the hayloft if Bill hadn't hauled them home every evening.

My husband and I were spared the parental purgatory of being cooped up in the cottage with a pair of crotchety ten-year-olds *and* a tempestuous toddler because the Yuletide Blight hadn't blighted Anscombe Manor. The antivirus force field that hovered over our cottage seemed to protect Emma's property as well, though she'd enhanced its effects by closing the riding school two weeks early and giving her hired hands ten unscheduled days of paid vacation.

Her isolation techniques weren't as extreme as Amelia's, but they produced similar results. Emma lived in the sprawling manor house with her husband, Derek, her grown stepchildren, Peter and Nell, and their spouses, Cassie and Kit, all of whom were as fit as fleas. As a construction expert who specialized in the restoration of historic buildings, Derek Harris had his own business to run, but since Peter, Cassie, Nell, and Kit knew their way around horses, Emma could depend on them—and on my horse-mad sons—to fill in for the stable hands.

Thanks to Emma and her blessedly healthy family, peace reigned in our home, or as much peace as could be expected with a nearly-two-year-old ruling the roost, but Bill and I weren't grateful to them for purely selfish reasons. We were pleased for our community as well. With the Nativity play's cancellation, the brightest light on Finch's foggy horizon was the annual Christmas party at Anscombe Manor. If it, too, had been canceled, Finch's collective cup of Christmas cheer would have been drained to the dregs.

Happily, Emma hadn't let us down. Her party would go ahead as planned, though on a more modest scale than usual since none of the Blight-struck villagers would attend. The news was like a breath of fresh air for those of us who weren't housebound. After doing our duty and behaving as we ought, we were in desperate need of a little frivolity.

Emma Harris's Christmas parties were as predictable as they

were enjoyable. They always took place a week before Christmas; they always started at five o'clock in the evening; and they never ended before midnight. My sons could cope with the late hours, but Bess wasn't an all-night raver, which was why Emma always made sure that one of the manor's many bedrooms would be fit for a sleepy princess.

A pre-Christmas Christmas dinner with roast goose and all the trimmings would be followed by an evening filled with convivial conversation, silly games, and the telling of tall tales around the great hall's roaring fire. Although Emma insisted on doing the bulk of the cooking, she gave the rest of us leave to bring finger foods that would be consumed by the insatiable before and after the sit-down feast.

My cheese straws always went over well, but I'd decided that desperate times called for extra effort. In the Year of the Blight, I was determined to surprise my neighbors with an appetizer I'd never made before, and spinach-and-goat-cheese tartlets seemed like just the thing.

As I bustled about my kitchen on Saturday morning, preparing the phyllo dough and the savory filling, I couldn't have known that my tartlets would be the least of the surprises that would make our annual gathering unforgettable.

Two

My tartlets turned out splendidly, so splendidly, in fact, that I had to give my menfolk a stern lecture to keep them from gobbling up the fruits of my labor before we left the cottage. After sealing my culinary masterpieces in fog-proof storage containers and threatening Bill and the boys with grievous bodily harm if so much as a crumb went missing while my back was turned, I repaired to the nursery to dress Bess in her party frock.

I loved my sons dearly, but I couldn't deny that it was more fun to play dress-up with a daughter. Bess looked like a rosy-cheeked Christmas angel in her red velvet dress, white tights, and black patent leather Mary Janes (with nonslip soles). Although I knew that the glossy red headband I threaded through her dark, silky curls wouldn't stay put for long, I had the satisfaction of seeing her in her complete ensemble while it was still complete.

Will and Rob planned to escape to the stables after Emma's feast, so they had my permission to dress down for the evening in flannel shirts, quilted vests, blue jeans, and mud-stained Wellington boots. Bill, too, went for a casual look, but his charcoal-gray cable-knit sweater and twill trousers were a little more sophisticated than the boys' barn-appropriate attire.

I opted to go full-on festive, with slim black trousers, a white silk blouse, a red velvet blazer, and a sparkly Christmas tree brooch the boys had made for me in their final art class before the holidays. The brooch was as garish as a Las Vegas billboard, but I wouldn't have dreamed of attending the party without it.

We were running late, as usual, but after filling Stanley's food and water bowls and assuring him that we'd be back before daybreak, we were ready to go. Will and Rob carried Bess's baby gear to our canary-yellow Range Rover, and Bill carried Bess, but I took charge of my tartlets, tucking the precious containers tenderly between the diaper bag and the bag containing Bess's mandatory supply of extra clothes as well as her favorite cuddly toy. Bianca the unicorn would, I thought, add a comforting touch of familiarity to the unfamiliar bedroom at Anscombe Manor.

Since the sun had set at four o'clock, we drove to the manor in a darkness rendered nearly impenetrable by drifting clouds of fog. The Rover's fog lights cast an eerie glow over the mist-cloaked hedgerows lining the narrow, twisting lane, making it seem as if we were caught in a cobwebbed tunnel filled with weirdly writhing wraiths.

A sense of claustrophobic dread would have assailed me if I hadn't grown accustomed to the uncanny shapes that floated through the strangely shifting gloom. Instead of quaking in my black leather ankle boots, I sat back, relaxed, and listened while my children discussed Thunder, Storm, and the gray pony Bess intended to ride when she was old enough to sit tall in the saddle. Bess's contribution to the conversation consisted mainly of repeating the word "hoss" at regular intervals, but I knew what she meant.

With characteristic attention to detail, Emma Harris had marked the turnoff to Anscombe Manor's winding drive with lanterns hung from tall, hooked spikes. She'd outlined the drive with lanterns as well, to keep her guests from veering off course and into four-bar fences, drainage ditches, and/or the lime trees she and Derek had planted to replace the azaleas that had originally bordered the drive. Azaleas, my sons had informed me, were poisonous to horses, but lime trees posed no threat to their health. Emma had provided further guidance for her guests by illuminating every window in the manor house.

If my father-in-law's stately home was a symphony of Georgian symmetry, Anscombe Manor was a concerto of quirkiness. On a clear day, it had the mongrel appearance of a building that had been altered over the course of several centuries by a succession of owners who couldn't agree on a prevailing style.

On a foggy night, it resembled a ghostly ship run aground on a storm-battered reef. The lights in its mismatched towers seemed to wink on and off as waves of fog broke over them, and the ground floor was enveloped in a rolling tide of mist.

The house had been in pretty bad shape when Emma and Derek Harris had moved into it, but they'd labored long and hard to turn it into a comfortable home. Anscombe Manor had entered the twenty-first century with, among other features, an enormous kitchen with a vaulted stone ceiling, a dining room large enough to accommodate a Victorian dinner party, a Tudor great hall with a hammer-beam roof, a Gothic library with a movable wrought-iron staircase, twelve bedrooms of widely varying shapes and sizes, and a collection of outbuildings that included a lovely nineteenth-century stable block made of honey-colored Cotswold stone.

The Harrises, too, had left their mark on the property. In addition to updating the interior infrastructure and replacing the roof, Derek had created apartments within the manor for his son and daughter and their respective spouses. When Emma had started her riding school, she'd embellished the grounds with a pair of outdoor riding rings, a modest indoor arena, and a manure pit that, on hot summer days, lent the estate an authentically medieval air.

The floodlights mounted on the manor's facade illuminated several cars parked on the graveled apron at the end of the drive. As we cruised cautiously around the final bend, I spotted the Buntings' black sedan, Mr. Barlow's paneled van, Bree Pym's almost-new Morris Mini, and Charles Bellingham's brand-new SUV, but the Hobsons' blue hatchback was missing.

"Where are James and Felicity?" I asked as Bill pulled in beside Bree's Mini.

"Maybe they're running late, too," he replied. "The fog may be worse near their cottage."

"It would have to be horrendous to make them later than us," I said. "We're always the last to arrive."

"Another fine tradition bites the dust," said Bill with an insincere sigh.

We unloaded the Rover, climbed the broad stone staircase, and crossed the flagstone terrace to the garlanded front door, where the boys took turns tugging on the bell pull until Derek Harris flung the door wide and greeted us with a merry "Ho, ho, ho!"

Derek was tall and lean and dressed as informally as my sons, though he wore leather work boots instead of wellies. He had a head full of curly salt-and-pepper hair, the weathered face of an outdoorsman, and stunningly beautiful sapphire-blue eyes. Derek had been a widower with two small children when he'd met and married Emma, but Peter and Nell never referred to Emma as their stepmother. She'd come into their lives when they'd needed her most, and from then on they'd regarded her as their mother.

"Come in, come in," Derek said, giving me a peck on the cheek and clapping Bill on the shoulder. "Hello, Bess! Learn any new words today? I hope you're hungry, boys. We've enough food to feed a cavalry regiment." After we followed him across the low-ceilinged vestibule to hang our coats and Bess's bags in the cloakroom, he relieved me of my storage containers and peered at them doubtfully. "What? No cheese straws?"

"I've raised my game this year," I said.

"So has Emma," said Derek. "Wait until you see the goose. It should be on the cover of a cooking magazine." When I reached for the containers, he shook his head. "I'll take your mystery munchies through to the kitchen, Lori. You and yours are wanted in the dining room. Everyone else is in there already, awaiting your arrival."

"Not everyone," I said. "Not unless James and Felicity hitchhiked."

"I'm sorry to say that the Hobsons won't be joining us tonight," said Derek. "James rang this morning to deliver the bad news."

"I hope they're not sick," I said.

"They're not, but their daughter and their grandchildren are," said Derek. "They've gone to Upper Deeping to give their son-in-law a helping hand."

"I'd expect nothing less of them," I said, "but it really is a shame. Felicity has earned a night out."

"So has James," said Bill. "Unfortunately, viruses don't share our sense of fair play."

"Let's hope it's the only bad news we hear all evening," I said.

"I don't think it will be," said Derek. Lowering his voice, he added, "Bree's looking stormy."

"Why?" I asked, intrigued.

"Don't know," he replied, "but I expect she'll tell us, now that you're here. Get thee to the dining room!"

He left for the kitchen and we obeyed his command.

The dining room had been expanded in Victorian times, and it retained its spacious proportions. Since Emma and Derek preferred clean lines to curlicues, however, they hadn't furnished the room in a fussy Victorian style. A few framed fruit-and-flower still lifes hung on the plain, pale walls, and the sole ornament on the mahogany sideboard was an old riding helmet. When set for the pre-Christmas feast, however, the immense mahogany table looked like an illustration from a Dickens novel.

The white damask tablecloth seemed to stretch for miles beneath gold-accented place settings that glittered in the light from a chandelier dripping with crystals. An Edwardian epergne overflowing with lacy ferns and red carnations took pride of place as the centerpiece, flanked by small silver vases filled with simple holly sprigs. Handwritten name cards in silver holders sat beside each place setting, a civilized solution to the scrum that would ensue if hungry guests were left to their own devices.

The only seasonal items missing from the table were Christmas crackers, explosive cardboard tubes wrapped in colorful paper and crammed with paper hats, cheap trinkets, and lame jokes. The tubes emptied with a bang when pulled at either end, at which point paper hats were donned, trinkets displayed, and lame jokes shared. Crackers were an essential feature of Yuletide celebrations in England, but Emma had decided long ago that some traditions should be reserved for Christmas Day.

Sixteen antique mahogany chairs and a thoroughly modern

high chair had been placed around the table, but no one was seated. Bree Pym and Lilian Bunting appeared to be engaged in a serious discussion in one corner of the room, while Charles Bellingham stood before the sideboard, regaling Theodore Bunting, Mr. Barlow, and Grant Tavistock with a funny story about an eccentric client. Not one member of the Anscombe Manor clan was present. I assumed that Peter, Cassie, Nell, and Kit were with Derek in the kitchen, helping Emma to put the finishing touches on her dishes.

The hum of conversation that had reached my ears in the vestibule came to an abrupt halt when we entered the dining room, and every head swiveled in our direction.

"Right," said Bill. "Who won?"

"I did!" crowed Lilian Bunting, waving a slip of paper in the air. "Half past five on the dot!"

Our customary tardiness had spawned a game that involved an old riding helmet filled with slips of paper inscribed with possible times of our arrival, none of which acknowledged the possibility that we might actually arrive on time. Lilian's triumphant cry brought a faint smile to Bree's troubled face and set off a roar of good-natured laughter among the others that was followed by a burst of greetings and the rumble of chair legs on the wooden floor as eager diners took their assigned seats.

Emma must have been listening for the rumble, because food and drink began to arrive almost as soon as we were seated. While Cassie filled our wineglasses and Nell filled our water glasses, Peter, Kit, and Emma filled the empty spaces on the damask tablecloth with a feast fit for a king.

Roast parsnips, turnips, carrots, and brussels sprouts; mashed potatoes with caramelized shallots; smashed potatoes roasted in goose fat; braised chestnuts; spiced red cabbage; rich, dark gravy; glistening cranberry sauce; and the bacon-wrapped miniature sausages known in England as pigs-in-blankets were but a few of the dishes that prefaced the arrival of a magnificent roast goose stuffed with apples and prunes and garnished with red currant jelly and creamy bread sauce.

Emma received shouts of acclaim and a round of applause when she finally took her place opposite Derek. The praise was well deserved because, although Emma was as American as I was, she'd mastered the art of traditional English cooking.

Had I spent untold hours toiling over a hot stove, I would have been a red-faced, sweaty mess, but apart from a slight frizziness in her graying dishwater-blond hair, Emma looked as fresh as a daisy. My ferociously organized friend had evidently given herself enough time to change from her kitchen duds into a tapestry blazer, a wine-colored turtleneck, and a pair of loose-fitting brown trousers that would forgive overindulgence.

The aromas wafting through the air were so seductive that I could scarcely keep myself from drooling while the vicar said grace, but once the chorus of "amens" had sounded, I dove headlong into the meal with a joyful abandon shared by my dining companions.

We knew how fortunate we were to be able to celebrate the season at Anscombe Manor, and when the plum pudding was brought, flaming, to the table, we joined Derek in a toast to absent friends.

Three

B ess was the first to leave the table. Having eaten her fill within the first thirty minutes of the goose's triumphant arrival, my daughter elected to work off her meal by toddling energetically around the dining room, stopping only to chat with a neighbor or to play with the wooden blocks Emma had provided for her amusement. No one complained about the noise she made. As Finch suffered from a severe shortage of little ones, Bess had, by default, become the village's baby girl.

Bree Pym said very little during dinner. Though conversation flowed freely once the initial feeding frenzy had subsided, she didn't speak unless spoken to, and even then her answers were brief and disjointed, as if she was too self-absorbed to pay attention to any topic other than the one that seemed to be troubling her. When I gave Lilian Bunting a querying look, she rolled her eyes heavenward and mouthed the word "later."

The feast drew to a close three hours after its tardy beginning. Peter and Kit gently ejected Emma from the dining room to prevent her from doing any more work, then stayed behind with Cassie and Nell to clear the table and to make up food parcels for our housebound neighbors. None of the leftovers from Emma's bounteous feast would go to waste.

Derek offered to transport the rest of us to the great hall in a wheelbarrow, but we managed to waddle across the vestibule without his assistance. Bill kept a firm hold on Bess's hand as we made our entrance, and I kept an eye on the boys, whose rapt expressions were the very essence of Christmastime.

The great hall was a sight to behold. A towering Christmas tree covered with colorful ornaments and topped with a gleaming gold star stood at the far end of the cavernous, oblong room. A pile of logs burned merrily in the Portland stone fireplace, and a pair of potted poinsettias flanked the Christmas cards that crowded the mantel shelf. Evergreen garlands dotted with tiny lights twinkled softly from the roof beams, wreaths hung from the oak-paneled walls, and silver bowls filled with walnuts and shiny apples graced the occasional tables placed here and there among the worn but comfy armchairs that had been grouped in cozy islands on the scattered Persian rugs.

To make the homely picture complete, the family's elderly black Labrador retriever snoozed in his plaid doggy bed near the fireplace. Hamlet raised his head when we came into the hall, and his tail thumped amiably, but we spared him the ordeal of meandering creakily around the room to greet each of us individually by gathering near his bed to give him a kind word and a cuddle.

Emma had shut out the foggy night by drawing the drapes over the row of tall mullioned windows that overlooked the curving drive and the sodden pastures in front of the manor house. A trestle table positioned before the windows held a Crock-Pot containing mulled wine, an insulated carafe filled with cinnamon-scented cider, and a cut-glass bowl brimming with the potent punch Derek concocted every year. Designated drivers bypassed Derek's punch completely, and the rest of us treated it with the respect it deserved.

The trestle table also held the snacks my neighbors and I had prepared for after-dinner munching, with the sweet offerings grouped on one side of the drinks, and the savory nibbles on the other. On the savory side, I spotted miniature quiches, sausage rolls, and meat pies; olive-stuffed flat bread cut into bite-size pieces; and an immense cheese ball coated with minced parsley and dotted with chopped pimientos. My tartlets seemed to beckon to me from a silver salver beside the cheese ball, but once I'd assured myself that they'd survived their journey without disintegrating, I ignored them.

Among the sweets were dainty mince pies; elegant petits fours; an abundance of gaily decorated cookies; and a platter piled with treats I couldn't identify. They appeared to be small balls of pale-brown dough, but I had no idea what they were called and I was too full to perform a taste test.

Will and Rob stuck around long enough to stuff their pockets with sausage rolls before they headed for the stables, but no one else showed the slightest interest in pillaging the food table. Lilian Bunting and Grant Tavistock were engrossed in a lively conversation about illuminated manuscripts; Bill, Derek, and the vicar discussed the weather's impact on Derek's business; and Mr. Barlow and Charles Bellingham exchanged views on a dwarf variety of euphorbia Charles hoped to add to his garden in the spring. Bree Pym, by contrast, stood alone beside Hamlet's doggy bed, gazing pensively into the fire.

Short, sturdy Mr. Barlow wore a white shirt and a red-and-green-striped tie with his second-best suit—his best was reserved for church. Though he was clearly enjoying his conversation with Charles, his eyes wandered toward Bree every so often.

I wasn't surprised. Mr. Barlow had taken Bree under his wing when she'd first arrived in Finch, and she'd taken a shine to him. If he needed help hanging a door, welding a tailpipe, or clipping the shrubs in the churchyard, Bree was the first person he called. He treated her like the son he'd never had, and she treated him like the father she wished she had. He was far too diffident to intrude on her thoughts, but I could see that he, too, was worried about her.

Bess was entranced by the Christmas tree. She seemed to be awed by it as well, which was a good thing, since it quelled her desire to play with the pretty ornaments. She allowed herself to be passed from one welcoming pair of arms to the next, but her gaze remained fixed on the tree. As soon as her eyelids began to droop, Bill signaled to me that he would be back in a moment, then carried our sleepy girl to the room Emma had readied for her.

Shortly after he left, Emma appeared at my elbow to stir the mulled wine. While she stirred, I gestured toward the unfamiliar dessert and asked who'd made it.

"I did," she replied. "They're an Indian sweet called besan ladoo."

"Since when do you make Indian sweets?" I asked, more impressed than ever by my friend's seemingly limitless fund of talents.

"Since last night," she replied. "The recipe was tucked into an old handwritten recipe book I found in the kitchen when we first moved into the manor. I was looking for something new to make this year, so I did a little research and discovered that besan ladoo are eaten during Indian festivals."

"Like Christmas?" I said doubtfully.

"Why not?" Emma rejoined. "Go ahead, try one. They may look a little drab, but they're delicious."

"I'm sure they are," I said, "but if I try one right now, I'll explode. Your besan ladoo will have to wait until my dinner has settled." Lowering my voice to a confidential murmur, I asked, "Do you know what's up with Bree?"

"Not a clue," said Emma, "but it must be something serious. She was in a funk when she got here, and she talked Lilian's ear off before dinner."

"Which means that Lilian must know what's going on," I said. "Let's ask her."

"Lilian!" Emma called. "Have a taste of my cider. I think I may have used too many cinnamon sticks."

"I doubt it," Lilian called back, but after making her apologies to Grant, she crossed to join us.

The vicar's wife was a slender, scholarly woman in her late fifties. Though she preferred to wear tweeds in winter, she'd dressed up for the evening in a tailored gray skirt suit with black velvet lapels. Her antique silver Christmas tree brooch provided a tasteful contrast to my sons' artistic creation.

To keep our cover story intact, Emma handed her a cup of cider, asking, "What do you think?"

"I think the cider's perfect," Lilian replied, without tasting a drop, "but it makes as good an excuse as any to get me over here so you can quiz me about Bree."

"Consider yourself quizzed," I said.

"Sorry," said Lilian. "I've taken a vow of silence. Bree wants to break the news herself."

"What's she waiting for?" I asked.

"She's waiting for the dishwashers to join us," Lilian replied. "Otherwise, she'll have to repeat her news, and it's not the sort of news she wants to repeat."

"She's not dying, is she?" I asked, glancing anxiously at Bree.

"My lips are sealed," said Lilian, contradicting herself by taking a sip of cider. "As I thought. Perfect."

I'll never know whether I could have badgered Lilian into spilling the beans about Bree, because at that moment, Peter, Cassie, Kit, and Nell entered the great hall, followed by Bill, who'd clipped the baby monitor to his belt. He'd evidently had no trouble persuading Bess to sleep in a room that was not her own.

Peter and Cassie Harris were in their late twenties, and compared with Kit and Nell, they were a charming but unremarkable couple. They'd traveled the world together before deciding that Peter's childhood home would be the best place to raise a family. To Emma and Derek's infinite delight, they were well on their way to starting one—their first child was due in April.

Kit and Nell Anscombe-Smith were unlike any couple I'd ever met. A grand opera could have been written about them, but only if the composer gave it the happiest of happy endings. By a strange twist of fate, Kit had, like Nell, grown up at Anscombe Manor. As a young man, he'd endured poverty, illness, and heartrending grief before another twist of fate brought him back to the manor to work as Emma's stable master.

Nell had been a schoolgirl at the time of his return, but she'd known from the first moment their eyes met that they were two halves of one soul. The age difference that troubled Kit meant nothing to Nell, who'd always been mature beyond her years. She was eighteen when yet another twist of fate enabled Kit to acknowledge his love for her, and they were wed. Their marriage had been as inevitable as it was sublime.

As if that weren't enough, they also happened to be two of the most beautiful creatures on God's green earth. Both were tall and slender, though Kit's feet touched the ground while Nell's seemed to glide gracefully over it. His short crop of prematurely gray hair gave him an air of gravity that softened when Nell's nimbus of guinea-gold curls came into view. Kit's violet eyes still made my heart melt, and Nell's ethereal loveliness still took my breath away. When they were together, it was hard to look anywhere else.

But it wasn't impossible. When they entered the hall with the others, my gaze went immediately to Bree Pym. The assembly had assembled. It was time for her to make her big announcement. I hoped fervently that it had nothing to do with her health.

Bree waited while the quartet of dishwashers were given a hearty cheer for volunteering to do the dirty work. She then turned her back to the fire and cleared her throat. Bree was just twenty-two and slightly built, with a heart-shaped face, expressive brown eyes, and short, spiky hair so dark it was almost black. Her nose ring glinted in the firelight, but the elaborate tattoos on her arms were hidden by the sleeves of a bulky navy-blue pullover that made her seem like a child dressed in a grown-up's clothing.

"Um," she said, and the room became silent save for the fire's crackle. "I don't tell you often enough how much you mean to me. I inherited a lot more than a house when I came to Finch. I inherited a family as well. *You're* my family, and I need to tell you something. I won't mind one bit if you pass it along to everyone else in Finch. It'll save me the trouble of breaking the same news over and over again." She thrust her hands into the pockets of her faded blue jeans, took a shaky breath, and said, with a slight quaver in her voice, "It's about Jack MacBride. You remember Jack, don't you?"

Heads nodded. We remembered Jack. He was a handsome Australian conservationist and Bree's fiancé. We loved Jack, but Bree was in love with him, or at least she had been the last time I'd checked.

"Jack rang me from Stockholm this morning," Bree continued. "Turns out he won't be here for Christmas. In fact, he won't be coming back here anymore. He's met someone else he loves better than me, a Swedish microbiologist who likes to travel as much as he does. Neither one of them wants to put down roots, and that's all I want to do, so it's for the best. Maybe I should have known that things wouldn't work out between us, but I didn't. There won't be the wedding you wanted, and I'm sorry for that, but"—with a nod at Cassie—"you have a christening to look forward to, and—"

The rest of her speech was cut short by the arms that enfolded her, one pair after another, hugging her, rocking her, assuring her without words that her family would be there for her, no matter what. The thought of her apologizing to us for the wedding Jack had canceled *with a phone call* brought tears to my eyes, but I held them back for her sake when my turn came to hug her.

"Enough!" Charles Bellingham roared, and everyone swung away from Bree to stare at him. Tall, portly, and balding, Charles was exquisitely attired in a crisp white dress shirt, black tuxedo trousers, a paisley smoking jacket, and a red satin bow tie, which he tweaked as he began, "Bree, my dear, I wish you'd found the man of your dreams—and I promise you, you will—but in the meantime, I refuse to allow a Swedish microbiologist to spoil your Christmas."

"So do I," said Grant Tavistock staunchly. Grant was shorter, slimmer, less bald, and less flamboyantly dressed than Charles, but he was no less chivalrous. "We'll throw a pity party for you after the holidays—"

"Oh, I *love* a good pity party," Charles interjected enthusiastically.

"—but right now we're going to cheer you up, whether you like it or not," Grant continued. "If we can't cheer you up, we can certainly distract you. Have you ever heard Charles yodel?"

"Yodel?" Charles said in alarm, giving Grant a sidelong look.

"I haven't heard him, either," Grant admitted, "but there's a first time for everything, as the actress said to the bishop." Like a ringmaster introducing a circus act, he extended an arm toward his partner and said, "Take it away, Charles!"

Even in the depths of her misery, Bree had to smile at the prospect of seeing a portly Englishman in a paisley smoking jacket make his yodeling debut. The prospect must not have appealed to Emma, however, because she came to her beleaguered guest's rescue.

"I have a better idea!" she said brightly.

"I can't think of a worse one," Charles muttered, sinking weakly into an armchair.

"As you know," Emma went on, "Cassie's baby is due in April."

"They'd have to be blind not to know it," said Peter, gazing proudly at his wife's blossoming figure.

Emma paused while a wave of affectionate chuckles rolled through the hall, then pressed on.

"As part of our preparations for the big day," she said, "Cassie and I have been hunting for a room that will make a suitable day nursery. Two weeks ago we found one room that will serve the purpose and another room that puzzled us. Derek and I have always used it as a storeroom, but once I cleared out the junk—"

"And donated it to the charity shop in Upper Deeping, where it has already brought in a tidy sum," I interrupted, raising a glass of mulled wine to Emma's generosity.

"Once I cleared out the junk and looked at the room with fresh eyes," Emma continued, brushing aside my compliment, "I couldn't figure out what its original purpose had been. Kit doesn't know, either."

Kit, who'd spent his childhood at Anscombe Manor, shook his head.

"Not a clue," he said. "We used it for storage, too. I'd never seen it empty until Emma cleared it out."

"It seems to me that, if we put our heads together, we might come up with an answer," said Emma.

"Of course we will," said Lilian Bunting. As a local historian, the vicar's wife took a lively interest in the local manor house.

"Take us to the room at once!" Grant demanded.

"Please do." Charles got to his feet and put an arm around Bree. "Solving a puzzle is a much better distraction than hearing me yodel, my dear."

"Much better for whom?" Bree asked slyly.

"For the civilized world," Charles declared.

"All right, then," said Emma. "Follow me."

Emma strode toward the vestibule and the rest of us trailed after her, but her house tour was nipped in the bud by Will and Rob, who barreled into the great hall, shouting excitedly.

"Mum! Dad! Come and see! The *fog* has turned to *ice!*"

Four

When the adults in the hall were slow to react, the boys clucked their tongues impatiently, scurried behind the trestle table, and pulled back the drapes.

"Look!" Rob entreated.

"Ice!" Will repeated, in case we hadn't heard him the first time.

With a wheeling maneuver that would have earned a severe reprimand from any self-respecting drill instructor, we rushed en masse to the windows to gaze, dumbfounded, at a landscape transformed from a horror film backdrop into a scene from a fairy tale.

The world beyond the wavy panes looked like a snow globe filled with glitter. At some point in the evening, the fog had lifted, the temperature had dropped, and the persistent drizzle had begun to freeze in midair. Sleet twinkled like tinsel as it fell from the sky, coating everything it touched in a crystalline carapace. Bathed in the hanging lanterns' pools of light, trees, fence rails, and pastures glowed with an otherworldly radiance. Enchanted, I half expected the Snow Queen to dash up the drive in a silver sleigh drawn by a prancing steed.

Mr. Barlow didn't share my starry-eyed vision.

"Just what we need," he said dourly. "An ice storm."

"I'll find out how bad it is," said Derek, heading for the vestibule.

"I'll come with you," said Mr. Barlow.

"So will I," said Bill, tossing the baby monitor to me.

"Be careful, Dad," Will cautioned.

"It's slippery," said Rob. "We fell three times—"

"—on our way in from the stables," Will concluded.

"Are you okay?" I asked, giving my sons a maternal once-over.

"Sure we are," said Rob. "It was fun!"

"Like a gigantic skating rink," said Will.

"Wish we'd brought our skates," Rob said wistfully.

"Wish I'd brought mine," I said, giving him a sideways hug.

I clipped the monitor to the waistband of my trousers, then turned my attention to the not-so-great outdoors as Bill, Derek, and Mr. Barlow came into view, bundled up to the eyeballs and walking as though they, too, wished they'd brought their skates. They crept gingerly across the floodlit terrace and clung to the balustrade as they descended the broad stone stairs. While Bill examined the parked cars, Derek and Mr. Barlow advanced slowly up the drive, stopping at each hanging lamp to take a closer look at the ice-covered gravel.

Indoors, Grant was the first among us to find his voice. "I didn't see this coming," he commented.

"Nor did I," said Lilian, "and I listened to the weather report before Teddy and I left the vicarage. Fog? Yes. Drizzle? Yes. Ice storm? Not one word of warning."

"It takes great courage to predict the weather in England," said the vicar, forgivingly. "Conditions change so rapidly that our forecasters are bound to get it wrong from time to time."

"They certainly got it wrong this time," said his wife, less forgivingly.

"Who made the goat cheese tartlets?" Charles asked.

"I did," I replied.

"They're scrumptious," he said, brushing telltale crumbs from his lips with a napkin. "Your cheese straws are good, Lori, but the tartlets are great. You should bring them every year."

"I'll bear it in mind," I promised, preening inwardly. "What did you bring?"

"The mince pies," he replied, "but I didn't make them. Henry looked so lonely in the tearoom that I bought some, just to keep him company."

"You can't go wrong with Sally's mince pies," I said.

"My thoughts exactly," said Charles. "In fact—"

"I hate to interrupt," Grant interrupted, nodding at the windows, "but Derek, Bill, and Mr. Barlow are coming back."

The intrepid explorers had regrouped on the terrace. After the front door opened and closed, the rest of us came out from behind the trestle table and stood before the fireplace to await their pronouncements. As the three men trooped into the great hall, still clad in their jackets, caps, and gloves, I could tell by the grim expression on Mr. Barlow's face and by the frost on Bill's eyelashes that the news wasn't going to be good.

"Well?" said Emma.

"No one's driving home tonight," Derek announced.

"The car doors are frozen shut," said Bill, "and you'll be taking your lives in your hands if you try to walk."

"It's slicker than whale snot out there," Mr. Barlow declared, provoking a snort of laughter from Bree, "and the frozen stuff is still coming down."

"Not to worry," Derek said briskly. "If the ice doesn't melt by morning, I'll use the tractor to spread sand and straw on the lane. It should give you enough traction to drive home safely."

"No use waiting for the county to do the job for us," Mr. Barlow observed. "They don't know Finch exists."

"And in the meantime?" Grant asked.

"In the meantime," said Derek, "I'd advise you strongly to stay here."

"No choice," said Mr. Barlow.

"I blame my wife," said Bill.

"Me?" I said, startled. "Why me?"

"You've already been snowbound by a blizzard and marooned by a flood," Bill said, referring to two unfortunate incidents in my past, one of which had occurred fairly recently. "It stands to reason that you'd be stranded by an ice storm next."

"You were marooned by the flood, too," I pointed out.

"I've never been snowbound," he countered. "Let's face it, Lori. You're a magnet for weather disasters."

"But we still love you," said Charles, and everyone, including me, laughed.

"You're more than welcome to stay the night," Emma said to her guests. "We have enough beds and bedrooms to go around, and—"

"Why do you have so many extra beds?" Grant inquired curiously.

"The stable hands have to sleep somewhere when the weather turns ugly," Emma replied. "Since we don't have a bunkhouse, they sleep in the manor."

"Lucky stable hands," said Grant.

"As I was saying," Emma continued, "I'm sure we can wrangle

up some pajamas and nightgowns for you to use. I can provide everyone with a new toothbrush as well." Before Grant could ask why she had so many new toothbrushes, she turned to him and explained, "I keep them on hand for our students to use before gymkhanas. Clean teeth make a good impression on judges."

"May we sleep in the stables, Mum?" Will asked, his brown eyes alight with gleeful anticipation.

"We left our sleeping bags here the last time we stayed over," Rob reminded me.

"You may sleep in the stables," I told them, "as long as you promise to take off your boots *before* you climb into your sleeping bags."

The boys high-fived each other, then hesitated, as if they'd realized that the ice storm might pose problems they hadn't envisaged.

"What about Stanley?" Will asked, turning to Bill. "Who'll feed him in the morning?"

"Stanley has plenty of water and a big bowl of dry food," Bill answered. "He'll survive the night without us."

"All of our pets will survive the night without us," Grant put in. "Truth be told, our pups could do with missing a meal or two. Charles insists on feeding them from the table."

"Dad feeds Stanley from the table," Will said with a sympathetic nod.

"Your father is a compassionate man," Charles said loftily.

"Will we go to church before we go home tomorrow?" Rob asked me.

I looked questioningly at the vicar. Tall, thin, and gray-haired, with a long, mournful face and a mild disposition, Theodore

Bunting gave Rob's question careful consideration before reply-ing, "Since every able-bodied member of the parish is here, we may as well hold the morning service here as well. With our hosts' permission, of course."

"Permission granted," said Derek.

"Are we agreed, then?" Lilian asked, surveying those of us who didn't live at the manor. "Shall we accept Emma's invitation to spend the night in Anscombe Manor?"

"Of course we shall, with heartfelt thanks," said Charles. "What fun! Our Christmas party has officially become a slumber party!"

Rob and Will thrust triumphant fists into the air before refill-ing their pockets with sausage rolls, collecting apples to give to the horses, and racing out of the great hall.

"Slow down on the ice!" I hollered after them. "And boots off before—"

"We *know*, Mum!" they hollered back.

There was a flurry of activity as everyone pitched in to make the bedrooms ready for occupancy. Bill and I elected to sleep in Bess's ground-floor room, but the others clambered up and down various staircases, carrying pillows, blankets, sheets, towels, new toothbrushes, and borrowed nightclothes to their chosen bed-chambers.

The exercise restored lost appetites. When we eventually reas-sembled in the great hall, no one ignored the food table. Even the designated drivers were free to avail themselves of the mulled wine and Derek's punch, though they exercised due caution with the latter.

My tartlets disappeared with gratifying speed, and Emma's

besan ladoo were a huge success. Though the Indian sweets resembled pale-brown balls of dough, Emma explained to anyone who asked that they were made of chickpea flour cooked with clarified butter, then mixed with white sugar and finely chopped nuts. She also explained that the recipe's simplicity had come as a relief after the rigors of preparing a complete Christmas dinner.

The ice storm made the great hall seem cozier than ever, but Mr. Barlow chose to stand near the windows, scanning the frozen world for the slightest sign of a thaw. Bree's young face became marginally less haggard as the evening progressed, and though she declined an invitation to play charades, she did her best to look as if our antics amused her. Mindful of her heartache, no one mimed romantic scenes.

It was nearing midnight when Mr. Barlow disrupted the proceedings.

"Will you look at that!" he exclaimed. "Some fool's coming up the drive!"

I peered past him through the windows and saw, blurred by needles of sleet, a pair of headlights advance at a snail's pace around the final bend.

A chorus of voices asked, "Who is it?"

"Don't know," said Mr. Barlow. "Looks like an old Peugeot. No one in Finch drives a Peugeot, but—" He broke off with a gasp. "Oh, my Lord, they've gone into a ditch."

Wordlessly, Derek and Bill ran after Mr. Barlow as he snatched up his jacket and dashed out of the great hall to give aid to the storm's first victim.

Five

Once the rapid-response team hit the ice, it couldn't afford to move rapidly. Clustered once more at the windows, we watched in anxious silence as Derek, Bill, and Mr. Barlow shuffled cautiously across the frozen terrace. Derek must have had a few flashlights close at hand, because three bright beams bobbed with excruciating slowness down the broad stone staircase and up the curving drive. It was the most languid rescue mission I'd ever witnessed.

The car had taken a nosedive into the drainage ditch. It sat lopsidedly, its rear end pointing upward, its headlights mired in mud. I couldn't tell a Peugeot from a pomegranate, but I could see by the glow of a hanging lantern that the small four-door sedan didn't belong to anyone I knew. I wondered who the driver was and why he'd braved the elements to come to Anscombe Manor.

"Should we ring the emergency services?" Grant asked.

"It'll take forever for an ambulance to get here," Charles pointed out.

"Let's find out if the driver's injured before we dial nine-nine-nine," Lilian advised. "We wouldn't want an ambulance crew to risk their lives for a false alarm."

"Even if the driver isn't injured," said the vicar, "he may be in shock."

"I'll fetch some blankets," said Cassie.

"I'll get the first-aid kit," said Kit.

"I'll put the kettle on," said Nell.

"An excellent notion," said Lilian, nodding at Nell. "A cup of strong, sweet tea is the best remedy for shock."

While the rest of us watched the drama unfold outdoors, Peter added logs to the fire, moved an armchair closer to the hearth, and placed a small round table beside the armchair. Hamlet raised his head to observe him placidly, then returned to doggy dreamland.

"They've reached the car," Grant narrated for Peter's benefit. "They've opened the door. They've extracted the driver."

"Extracted?" Peter said in alarm.

"They've helped him to climb out of the car and the ditch," Grant clarified. "He doesn't seem to be hurt. Correction: *She* doesn't seem to be hurt. She can walk, at any rate."

"Any passengers?" Peter asked.

"They haven't pulled anyone else out of the car," Grant informed him.

The driver appeared to be a short, plump woman, but I couldn't tell whether she was young, old, or middle-aged. Derek and Bill offered their strong arms to steady her as they began their slow-motion journey back to the manor, and she clung to them as if her legs had turned to jelly.

Mr. Barlow stayed behind with the car. After crouching low to examine the undercarriage, he straightened, shook his head, and crawled through the driver's-side door to retrieve a black purse from wherever it had landed. He then popped the trunk and removed a small suitcase. After closing the trunk and the door, he trudged behind the trio, toting the purse and the suitcase. He'd clearly decided that the car was too damaged to drive.

"It looks as though you'll have another guest at your slumber party, Emma," Charles commented.

"Not a problem," she said. "I'm just glad she didn't slide off the road in a spot where no one could help her."

"Perish the thought," the vicar said with a shudder.

Kit returned with the first-aid kit, and Cassie followed him with two red-and-gray-striped wool blankets draped over her forearms. They crossed to stand beside me at the windows while Derek and Bill guided the luckless driver up the perilous stairs.

"I don't recognize her," said Cassie.

"She's not from Finch," said Peter, taking the blankets from his blossoming wife. "And she's not one of our students."

"I don't think she's one of our parents, either," said Cassie.

"Who is she, then?" said Kit. "And what brought her to Anscombe Manor?"

"I've been asking myself the same questions," I said.

"She'll answer them soon enough," Grant said, and as he turned to face the vestibule, the rest of us turned with him.

Derek and Bill towered over their damsel in distress as they escorted her into the great hall. She was at least a foot shorter than they were, and she was definitely middle-aged. Her round face was lined with a faint web of wrinkles, but apart from a dab of lipstick, she wore no makeup. She was dressed plainly but neatly in a black beret, a knee-length black wool coat, black tights, and extremely sensible black rain boots. Her tightly curled iron-gray hair stuck out around the edges of her beret like lamb's-wool trim.

She drew a dainty white handkerchief from her coat pocket with a trembling hand and dabbed at her red nose while she apologized to her saviors.

"I'm s-sorry to be such a b-bother," she stammered through chattering teeth. "I'm sorry to put you to so much t-trouble."

"There's nothing to be sorry about," said Derek.

"You're safe now," Bill assured her.

"Let me take your hat and coat," said Emma, stepping forward.

When the woman fumbled with her coat buttons, Emma undid them for her, then removed both coat and beret, passing them to Derek. Before Peter wrapped a striped blanket around the woman's shoulders, I caught a glimpse of a white blouse with a Peter Pan collar, a baggy black cardigan, and a black wool skirt. Her only adornment was an intricately carved jet brooch pinned like a cameo at her throat.

"Do f-forgive me," the woman was saying. "It's entirely m-my fault. I was on my way to Tewkesbury, but I must have taken a wrong t-turn. I saw your lights and I thought perhaps you might be able to p-point me in the right direction, but now, oh, dear, I d-don't know what I'll do."

"Are you hurt?" Emma asked, studying the woman's face intently, as if searching for cuts or bruises. "Did you bump your head?"

"No, indeed," the woman replied. "It was a slow-motion accident. I had ample time to b-brace myself, and I always wear my seat belt. Well, not always, because it would be impossible to w-walk if I wore it all the time, but I always wear it when I drive. My shoulders may be a bit sore tomorrow, but I haven't b-broken anything." The woman put a hand to her cheek and peered at us worriedly. "Am I babbling? I think I must be b-babbling. Do forgive me."

"There's nothing to forgive," Emma said soothingly, steering her newest houseguest toward the fireplace. "Come and sit by the fire. We need to warm you up. Poor thing—your hands are like ice."

"Oh, dear," the woman said as her wondering gaze traveled around the great hall. "I've c-crashed your party." She gave an unsteady giggle. "Literally as well as f-figuratively."

"Humor in the face of adversity," the vicar said with an approving nod.

"It may be closer to hysteria than to humor," the woman told him as Emma eased her into the armchair. "I f-feel quite strange."

"Of course you do," said Emma, chafing the woman's pink hands. "Can you tell me your name?"

"It's Trout," the woman said, and her round face grew as pink as her fingers.

"Are you sure you're okay, Mrs. Trout?" Emma asked.

"No," the woman said instantly. "That is, I'm fine, but I'm not . . . I've never been . . . What I mean to say is: It's miss. Miss Trout. Miss Matilda Trout." She sighed. "But everyone calls me T-Tilly."

"Tilly Trout?" said Charles, with a glimmer of a smile.

Grant elbowed him in the ribs, but Tilly, who'd seen Charles's reaction, seemed unfazed by it. If anything, she seemed to expect a roomful of strangers to treat her name as a joke.

"Dreadful, isn't it?" she said with a resigned air. "I was named after an aunt. I'm sure my parents meant well, but I rather wish Aunt Tilly had taken her name to the g-grave with her."

"I'm overjoyed that she didn't," said Charles. "Your name is as delightful as it is distinctive. I wouldn't change a syllable."

"I would," said Tilly.

"I'm Emma Harris," said Emma, tucking the second blanket around Tilly's lap, "and I hope you'll call me Emma. My family and I live here, at Anscombe Manor."

"Anscombe M-Manor?" said Tilly. "Is that where I am?"

"It is," Emma replied. "You're not far from Tewkesbury, but yes, you did take a wrong turn—an easy mistake to make on a night like this. Where do you live, Tilly?"

"Oxford." Tilly's shoulders sank despondently. "I should n-never have left."

"You couldn't have known what would happen," Emma said consolingly. "The ice storm took us by surprise, too." She glanced over her shoulder as Nell glided gracefully into the hall, carrying a silver tea tray set with a bone china tea service and a big red mug. "Here's Nell with your tea, Tilly."

Tilly's mouth fell open when she caught sight of Nell. She wasn't the first, nor would she be the last, to be stunned by Nell's radiant beauty.

"My g-goodness," Tilly murmured dazedly, "you're like an angel. If I weren't so c-cold, I'd think I'd died and gone to heaven."

Nell didn't help matters by smiling beatifically as she placed the tea tray on the round table beside Tilly's chair, but she brought the conversation back down to earth by saying, "You're very kind, but if you look closer, you'll see that I have no wings."

Tilly returned Nell's smile sheepishly, accepted a mug of strong, sweet, milky tea, and took a prolonged sip.

"Heavenly," she said when she came up for air. "Wings or no wings, you *are* an angel."

The sovereign remedy worked its usual magic. By the time Tilly placed the empty mug on the tea tray, her hands had stopped shaking, her teeth had stopped chattering, and she seemed a little more composed.

"Is there someone you'd like us to call?" Emma asked.

"No, there's no one," said Tilly. Her eyebrows shot up and her expression changed with almost comical speed as she revised her answer. "Yes! Yes, there is! How could I be such a dunderhead? I should ring the hotel in Tewkesbury to let them know I'll be late. They'll be expecting me, and I wouldn't want them to worry. I have the number here somewhere." She gazed at her empty hands, then patted the blankets, as if she thought the phone number might be hidden beneath them.

"Here you go," said Mr. Barlow, presenting Tilly with the purse he'd taken from her car. It reminded me of the leather purse my late mother had carried to church on Sundays—black and rectangular, with a gold-colored clasp and a pair of short leather handles. Not fancy, but respectable.

"Thank you," said Tilly, beaming at Mr. Barlow. "Thank you for rescuing my purse—and me!" After a quick search, she came up with a small brown notebook, which she opened to the first page. "Here it is: The Royal Hop Pole, on Church Street." She resumed her search. "Now, where did I put my mobile?"

"Relax," said Cassie, plucking the notebook gently from Tilly's grasp. "I'll ring The Royal Hop Pole for you."

"I'd be very grateful if you would," said Tilly. "I'd probably start babbling again. Please tell them that I don't know when I'll be able to get to Tewkesbury. I'm afraid I've broken a strut."

"A strut?" said Emma, peering confusedly at Tilly's legs.

"She's talking about her car," Mr. Barlow clarified. "What makes you think you've broken a strut, Miss Trout?"

"I felt a disturbing tug on the steering wheel during my accident," Tilly replied, "and my car seemed to sag oddly after it came to rest in the ditch. It could be any number of things, but I suspect a broken strut." She winced uneasily. "Perhaps two broken struts. My car is rather old. Is there a repair shop nearby?"

Mr. Barlow, who had listened with interest to Tilly's diagnosis, said, "Don't you fret, Miss Trout. I'll haul your car to my place in the morning. You may have a busted strut or two, but I won't know for sure until I can get her up on blocks."

"Are you a mechanic?" she asked.

"I used to be one," he replied, "but I've kept my hand in since I retired."

"Mr. Barlow is a brilliant mechanic," Bree said staunchly. "We all depend on him."

"Then I shall depend on Mr. Barlow, too," said Tilly.

I expected Mr. Barlow to mutter, "No choice," but he colored to his roots and said nothing as he placed Tilly's suitcase next to her chair. Like her purse, it was serviceable rather than showy.

"You saved my suitcase as well," said Tilly, favoring Mr. Barlow with another smile. "Thank you. Perhaps you can direct me to the nearest hotel."

"The Peacocks rent a couple of rooms above their pub," said Mr. Barlow, "but they're too sick to play innkeeper."

"Even if they weren't," said Emma, "we wouldn't send you out in this weather, Tilly. You'll spend the night with us."

"We're all spending the night here," I said cheerfully. "It's our first annual Christmas dinner and pajama party."

"If you're all staying," said Tilly, "you can't possibly have enough room for me."

"Yes, we can," said Derek. "We have quite a few bedrooms, and one of them will be yours for as long as you need it."

Tilly's lower lip quivered and her gray eyes filled with tears. She might have broken down under the weight of so much benevolence if Emma hadn't asked her when she'd last eaten.

"I had a bowl of soup before I left home," said Tilly, wiping her eyes with her handkerchief. "I intended to have dinner at the hotel, but—" She broke off, looking utterly woebegone.

"I'll fix a plate for you," said Emma. "You'll feel better after you've had a proper meal." When Tilly began to get to her feet, Emma restrained her. "Stay where you are. I'll bring you a tray."

Lilian and I exchanged meaningful glances, then accompanied Emma to the cavernous kitchen. She didn't need our assistance to assemble a proper meal from her copious leftovers, but we felt an urgent need to discuss her unexpected houseguest. Gossip was depressingly thin on the ground in Finch.

"Are you sure Tilly didn't hit her head?" I asked Emma. "She seems a bit disoriented."

"According to Bill," Emma said dampingly, "you seemed addled after you drove your car into the ditch in front of Bree's house. And you didn't hit your head."

"One accident," I said with an exasperated groan. "I have one measly accident umpteen years ago and Bill can't stop talking about it."

"I would have called for an ambulance if I thought Tilly had a concussion," said Emma, "but I don't believe she does. I couldn't run a riding school without knowing the symptoms. Her speech isn't slurred, she remembers the accident clearly, she's not sensitive to light or noise, she hasn't vomited, she doesn't seem to be nauseous, and she's making as much sense as she can, considering the circumstances. She's shaken, but she's not concussed."

"I suspect she's suffered a loss," Lilian said thoughtfully.

"What kind of loss?" I asked.

"The loss of someone close to her," Lilian replied, "perhaps a family member. I can't be certain, of course, but she's dressed rather somberly and she's wearing a jet brooch."

"I noticed the brooch," I said, putting a hand to my throat. "I've seen similar brooches in antique shops. They're always Victorian."

"Queen Victoria made jet jewelry fashionable," said Lilian. "She draped herself in it after Prince Albert's untimely death, and those who could afford to follow her example did so. Wearing jet to signify mourning is an old-fashioned custom, but Tilly strikes me as an old-fashioned woman."

"You may be onto something," I said, feeling a stab of pity for Tilly. "Remember when she said there was no one we could call for her, apart from the hotel? She's traveling solo, too. The death, if there was one, may have left her alone in the world."

"A recent loss would explain her navigational error," Lilian reasoned.

I nodded. "She could have taken the wrong turn because she was overwhelmed with grief."

"Before you kill off Tilly's friends and relations," Emma said dryly, "you might try asking her if she's suffered a loss."

"I shall ask her," said Lilian, "but not tonight."

"Not unless she brings it up," I put in. "If she wishes to share her burden, we'll be there for her."

"It would be unkind not to listen to her," Lilian added virtuously.

"Of course it would," Emma said, rolling her eyes. "In the meantime, you might try listening to someone who really has suffered a loss."

I stared at her blankly for a moment, then banged a fist against my forehead, exclaiming, "Bree! I forgot about Jack MacBride dumping Bree! I must be the worst friend in the history of friends."

"I forgot about her troubles, too," said Lilian with a rueful grimace. "What shall we do about Bree?"

"I'm sure you'll come up with something," said Emma, "but for now, let's feed Tilly."

Emma arranged cutlery, a cloth napkin, and the heaping plate of leftovers on a wooden tray and lifted it from the table. To disguise the real reason for our retreat to the kitchen, I took a glass pitcher from a cupboard and filled it with water, and Lilian extracted a clean glass from the dishwasher.

"Feeble," Emma said scornfully, but though she had no trouble seeing through our ruse, I hoped it would fool Tilly Trout. Tilly had yet to learn that, in Finch, gossip was a way of life.

We returned to the great hall to find Cassie explaining to Tilly that The Royal Hop Pole's owner had agreed to cancel her hotel reservation without penalizing her. Apparently, the ice storm had engulfed Tewkesbury, too.

Nell made room for the wooden tray by moving the silver one to another table, Kit shifted the round table so that it sat in front of the armchair, and Emma set Tilly's meal before her. Lilian and I added our contributions and stood back.

"Thank you," said Tilly. "I feel as if Christmas has come early." She spread the napkin over her lap, then glanced self-consciously at the circle of faces surrounding her.

"Let Miss Trout eat in peace, will you?" Mr. Barlow said gruffly. "You'll give her indigestion, gawping at her like that."

Like chastened schoolchildren, we ducked our heads and, with mumbled apologies, shifted en masse from the fireplace to the Christmas tree, making a concerted effort not to look in Tilly's direction.

"Sardines?" Emma suggested, referring to an English version of hide-and-seek. "Treasure hunt? Blindman's bluff?"

"Would you mind very much if Teddy and I begged off?" said Lilian. "We're sorry to be party poopers, but it's well past our bedtime."

"It's past ours, too," said Peter, putting a protective arm around his wife.

"I tire more easily these days," Cassie admitted apologetically.

"We'll excuse ourselves as well," said Nell, taking Kit's hand.

He curled his fingers through hers and explained, "We have to be up with the birds to feed the horses."

"Sleep well, one and all," said Emma. "We'll see you"—she glanced at her watch—"later this morning."

The early-to-bed brigade said their good-nights and vacated the hall, leaving the rest of us to carry on without them.

"To tell you the truth," said Grant, "I'm not in the mood for games."

"I'm not in the mood to sing carols, either," said Derek.

"I'm not going to bed," I said stubbornly.

"Well, then," said Emma, "what shall we do next?"

Mr. Barlow, who'd seated himself in a chair beside Tilly's, called over his shoulder, "Here's an idea, Emma: Go and look at that peculiar room of yours, and take everyone with you. If Miss Trout needs anything, I'll get it for her."

His proposal was greeted with an enthusiastic murmur of approval.

"The ayes have it," said Emma. "Follow me!"

Six

The peculiar room was tucked away at the end of a gloomy oak-paneled corridor on the ground floor. Its carved oak door blended in so well with the paneling that I would have walked past it if Emma hadn't brought our procession to a halt. Even the doorknob was made of pitch-black oak.

"Here we are," Emma announced.

"Wait," I said as she reached for the doorknob. "Lilian's going to kill us when she finds out that we came here without her. Should I run upstairs and fetch her?"

"Let her sleep," Emma advised. "The room's not going anywhere. I can give her a private showing tomorrow."

"It won't be the same," I warned. "She'll miss out on the what's-the-room-for contest."

"She's married to a vicar. She's required by law to forgive us," Charles said, adding impatiently. "Are we going in or not?"

"I'll get the lights," said Emma.

She opened the door, stepped across the threshold, and touched a wall switch. Six brass wall sconces came on all at once, three on one side of the room and three on the other.

"I wired the sconces for electricity after we moved into the manor," Derek informed us. "Originally, they would have held candles."

The rest of us said nothing as we followed Emma to the center of the room, craning our necks to see what there was to see.

There wasn't much. The sconces cast a warm glow over a windowless oblong chamber with a decorative plaster ceiling and an elegant parquet floor. Though Emma and Derek had used it for storage, the ceiling, the floor, and the fine, head-high linenfold wainscoting suggested to me that it had once served a more exalted purpose.

"The Anscombe family owned the manor house for a few centuries before Derek and I bought it," Emma explained, "and the Mandeville family owned it before the Anscombes. I searched the house archives for an architectural plan that might indicate how the room was used in the past, but the ones I found simply identify it as a 'room,' if they identify it at all."

"When was it built?" asked Bill.

"The Mandevilles built this part of the manor house in the mid-sixteenth century," said Emma. "It's Tudor, like the great hall. If the first Queen Elizabeth had visited the Mandevilles, she could have held court in here."

"Good Queen Bess would never have held court in a room like this," Charles scoffed. "For one thing, it's too small to accommodate a royal retinue, and for another, it's too claustrophobic." He shuddered expressively. "I feel as if I'm standing in a giant's coffin."

"I was making a point about its age, Charles, not its purpose," said Emma. "I'm open to other suggestions."

"It could have been used as a bowling alley," Grant said tentatively.

"A sixteenth-century bowling alley?" I said, eyeing him doubtfully.

"I'm referring to lawn bowling," Grant clarified, "not the mechanized modern sport." Having won Finch's lawn bowling championship for three years running, he was regarded as something of an authority on the subject. "I know nothing of the mechanized version," he continued, "but I do know that lawn bowling predates the Tudor era. A bowling green in Southampton dates back to 1299."

"A medieval bowling alley?" I said. "I'm amazed."

"Bowling was so popular during Henry VIII's reign that he banned commoners from playing it," Grant went on. "He wanted them to concentrate on tilling the soil and practicing archery with the longbow. Aristocrats, on the other hand, were allowed to bowl whenever the fancy took them."

"Sir Francis Drake insisted on finishing a game before he sailed off to defeat the Spanish Armada," Charles put in.

"The Sir Francis Drake story may be apocryphal," Grant said, smiling, "but it illustrates the game's immense popularity. Lawn bowling usually takes place outdoors, on a bowling green, but the Mandeville family could just as easily have played it in a custom-built room."

"A rainy-day bowling alley for an aristocratic family?" said Charles, surveying the room. "Why not?"

"Because it's too fancy," I objected. "That's why not. Look around. Would you line the walls of a bowling alley with expensive linenfold panels?" I shook my head. "If bowlers used this room, the wainscoting would be broken or dented."

"It's neither," said Derek. "It hasn't been patched up, either. I inspected the woodwork after Emma emptied the room. Apart from a few scratches, it's as pristine today as it was when it was first installed."

"I rest my case," I said.

"Brava, Madam Barrister," Charles said huffily. "The world awaits your learned opinion."

"I don't have a one," I replied, ignoring his sarcasm. "It feels like a sensory deprivation chamber to me, but I don't think such a thing existed in Tudor times. Not unless you count dungeons, and I've never seen a dungeon with linenfold wainscoting and a parquet floor."

"No one has," Derek said dryly. "Dungeons tend to be a little less refined."

"So . . . not a throne room, not a coffin, probably not a bowling alley, definitely not a sensory deprivation chamber, and absolutely not a dungeon," said Emma, ticking the guesses off on her fingers. "We've ruled out five possibilities, but we haven't ruled anything in. More suggestions, please."

"Bomb shelter?" Bree ventured.

If Jack MacBride hadn't stomped on Bree's heart and left her to pick up the pieces, I would have been certain that she was joking. As it was, I didn't allow myself to chuckle until a weak smile appeared on her face. Her facetious guess had, however, inspired Bill to come up with a serious one.

"It could be a strong room," he proposed. "No windows, only one door, oak-paneled, buried at the back of the house . . . It fits the profile of a strong room."

"What's a strong room?" Bree asked.

"A room where valuables were kept," Bill replied. "Gold,

silver, spices, tea—high-priced items that might be targeted by thieves. I've never seen a strong room as large as this, but I suppose it could have been designed to allow the family to hide in here with their treasures if the house came under attack."

"So it could have been a bomb shelter," said Bree, looking astonished. "I was kidding."

"It's the likeliest idea I've heard so far," said Bill.

"Any others?" Emma requested.

Heads were scratched, chins were rubbed, and feet were shuffled, but no one spoke until a timid voice asked, "May I come in?"

I turned to see Tilly Trout standing in the doorway. Mr. Barlow stood behind her, his arms folded and his lips set in a thin, disapproving line.

"You may both come in," said Emma.

"The more the merrier!" said Derek.

"I don't mean to intrude," Tilly said as she and Mr. Barlow joined us, "but while I was enjoying the excellent meal you so thoughtfully prepared for me, Emma—your cranberry sauce is the best I've ever tasted, and the goose was so tender I could cut it with a spoon!—Mr. Barlow told me about the peculiar room. I must admit that my curiosity was piqued. When I'd consumed the last morsel—I didn't realize how hungry I was until I began eating!—I asked him if I, too, might see the room."

"I wanted her to stay off her feet," Mr. Barlow grumbled, "but she wouldn't listen."

"How did you know where we were?" Emma asked. "You've never been in this part of the house before, have you, Mr. Barlow?"

"No, I haven't," he answered, "but a deaf man could've heard you lot jabbering."

"We followed the sound of your voices," said Tilly, polishing Mr. Barlow's rough reply. "Would you mind very much if I examined the room, Emma? It's Tudor, isn't it?"

"No, I don't mind, and yes, it's Tudor," said Emma. "Feel free to speculate about why it was built. We've run out of plausible ideas."

"I haven't," Bill murmured, holding fast to his strong-room hypothesis.

Tilly strolled away from us to the far end of the room, opposite the door. She paused once before a wall sconce, paused again to gaze at the floorboards, and paused a third time to peer at the ceiling.

"Yes," she murmured, "it's as I thought."

"What's as you thought?" I asked. "Don't tell me you've worked out a solution."

"I believe I have," said Tilly.

"It's a strong room, isn't it?" Bill said.

"A strong room?" Tilly shook her head. "Oh, no, it's not a strong room. It's a chapel."

"A chapel?" Emma said incredulously.

"What makes you think it's a chapel?" Bill asked.

"The evidence," Tilly replied succinctly. She tilted her head back to gaze upward. "There's the hole in the ceiling where the sanctuary lamp hung."

"I've never noticed a hole," said Derek.

"It's been plastered over," Tilly explained, "but if you know where to look—"

"Show me." Derek crossed to her side in three strides and gazed intently at the ceiling directly above her head. "Ah, yes, I see it now, the slight indentation where the plaster's shrunk over time."

"You could probably poke your finger through it," said Tilly, "but I hope you won't. It would spoil the plasterwork."

"How did you know where to look?" he asked.

She pointed at the floor. "Do you see the worn spots, indicating that something heavy was dragged across the floor repeatedly? They were made by the legs of a table that was used as an altar. Where there's an altar, there must also be a sanctuary lamp."

"I see the worn spots," Derek conceded, "and I agree that a table must have made them, but I'm not as certain as you are that the table was used as an altar."

"You will be," she said serenely. She raised her voice slightly as she addressed the rest of us. "If I might draw your attention to the wall sconces? It doesn't matter which one. They're identical."

We scattered like pinballs and came to rest in six little groups, one before each of the sconces. Bill, Bree, and I studied ours dutifully. The curved arm that supported the electrified candleholder was quite plain, but the flat piece of metalwork that formed the backplate was inscribed with a floral pattern. I found the pattern attractive, but its significance eluded me.

"If you look very closely at the entwined rose stems in the incised design," said Tilly, "you'll see that they are, in fact, a stylized representation of crossed keys."

I stood on tiptoe to examine the inscribed backplate more closely, then nodded. "You're right, Tilly. Now that you've pointed them out, I can see the crossed keys."

A murmur of general agreement rumbled through the room.

"The crossed keys symbolize the keys to the kingdom of heaven, promised to Peter the apostle by Christ," said Tilly.

"Peter was the first Roman Catholic pope, wasn't he?" said Charles.

"He was," Tilly confirmed. "In the Roman Catholic Church, the crossed keys represent the pope's authority."

"I'm guessing it wasn't an Anglican chapel," said Grant.

"It most certainly was not," said Tilly.

"If it's a Roman Catholic chapel," I said, "why is it so plain?"

"It's all to do with the English Reformation." Tilly's brow furrowed slightly, then cleared as she said helpfully, "I can recommend several excellent works on the subject."

"Can you give us a condensed version?" I asked.

"I can, but even a condensed version is complicated," Tilly demurred. "I don't wish to be a bore."

"I'm not bored," I said, eager to gauge the depth of her knowledge. "Is anyone bored?"

"Not in the least," Derek said gallantly, and the others murmured encouraging words, except for Mr. Barlow, who looked as though he would have preferred to see Tilly resting before the fire in the great hall.

"Very well." Tilly clasped her hands together like a schoolmarm reciting the times table and went on with a confidence she hadn't shown in the great hall. "When Henry VIII parted ways with the Roman Catholic Church, he established the Church of England as a state religion with the monarch as its head. Those who remained faithful to Roman Catholic beliefs and practices were regarded as traitors, because they pledged their allegiance to the pope rather than to the English monarch."

"Did Queen Elizabeth—the first one—regard them as traitors, too?" Emma asked.

"I'm afraid she did," said Tilly. "She enforced her father's anti-Catholic laws and added some of her own. For instance, she made attendance at Church of England services compulsory. Those who refused to attend were punished."

"How?" I asked.

"Roman Catholics were not allowed to inherit or to purchase land," said Tilly, "and the land they already owned could be confiscated by the Crown. They couldn't hold public office or serve in the military or receive degrees from the universities in Oxford and Cambridge. In far too many cases, they were imprisoned, tortured, and put to death. Take the case of Margaret Clitherow, for example."

"Who is Margaret Clitherow?" Emma asked.

"Margaret Clitherow was a butcher's wife in York," said Tilly. "She was raised in the Protestant religion, but she converted to Roman Catholicism in 1574. She was later arrested for the crime of harboring fugitive priests in her home. Since it was a capital offense to harbor Roman Catholic priests, she was crushed to death on Lady Day 1586."

"I'm almost afraid to ask," I said, "but what does it mean to be crushed to death?"

"Margaret Clitherow was stripped down to her shift," Tilly replied, blushing faintly and averting her eyes from the men in the room. "She was forced to lie on her back with a sharp rock positioned beneath her spine. A door from her own house was then placed on top of her. Heavy weights were piled upon the door until the sharp rock broke her spine. She died within fifteen minutes, but her mangled body was left beneath the weighted door for a full six hours."

"It's barbaric," said Emma, looking queasy.

"When Queen Elizabeth was informed of the execution, she, too, was horrified by its barbarity," said Tilly, "but her anti-Catholic laws made it possible."

"I'll never call her Good Queen Bess again," Charles said, clucking his tongue in disgust.

"She was good in many ways," Tilly said hastily, "but she was also at war with Spain, a Roman Catholic country closely allied with the pope. The Spanish were determined to restore the Roman Catholic Church in England and to replace Elizabeth with a Roman Catholic monarch. In concert with the pope, they created a network of spies—and it must be admitted that many of them were priests—to undermine her sovereignty. Elizabeth couldn't afford to show mercy to those who aided and abetted the enemy in a time of war. She passed stringent anti-Catholic laws for secular as well as for spiritual reasons."

"They must have been repealed at some point," I said.

"Anti-Catholic penal laws remained on the books in England until 1829," Tilly said, "though the most extreme punishments were no longer enforced by then."

"Thank goodness for small blessings," Emma muttered. She cast a haunted look around the peculiar room. "And thank you, Tilly. I think I understand why the chapel is . . . understated."

"It was inadvisable to advertise one's allegiance to the church of Rome during the Tudor period in England," said Tilly. "If Roman Catholic families wished to avoid persecution, they practiced their faith privately in rooms that could not readily be identified as places of worship." She pointed to the ceiling. "The sanctuary lamp could be removed in a trice." She pointed at the worn spots on the floor. "The altar could be pushed against the wall." She pointed at a sconce. "The only permanent symbols of the Roman Catholic faith were cleverly disguised as the stems of Tudor roses."

Charles turned to Emma. "You have your answer, Emma. The peculiar room was a clandestine Roman Catholic chapel."

"The Mandevilles must have been Roman Catholics," said Emma, "because the Anscombes were staunch Anglicans."

"May I ask who the Mandevilles and the Anscombes are?" Tilly inquired.

"The Mandevilles built this part of the manor house," Emma explained, "and the Anscombes lived in the manor after them."

"'Mandeville' is a Norman name," Tilly said reflectively. "Many of the old Norman families refused to renounce their faith. The Crown could have appropriated the manor house from the Mandevilles and awarded it to the Ansc—" She broke off and quickly covered her mouth as a yawn overtook her.

"Enough," Mr. Barlow declared. "You can save the rest of your questions for the morning. Miss Trout needs her sleep. Show her to her room, will you, Emma?"

Since Tilly's yawn had triggered a general outbreak of yawns, no one argued with Mr. Barlow. We thanked Tilly and bade her good night as Emma escorted her from the chapel, but we said little else as we made our way to our respective bedrooms. It was half past two in the morning and we were all ready to turn in.

My baby girl needed a diaper change, but she barely woke for it. I blessed her sleepy little head as I donned a borrowed night-gown and crawled into bed beside Bill.

"A Christmas party we won't soon forget," he remarked.

"Not in a month of Sundays," I agreed. "How does it feel to be a hero?"

"Sleepy," Bill replied.

"I wonder if Tilly Trout is a historian," I said.

"Could be," said Bill, snuggling into his pillow.

"Can you believe what happened to Bree?" I said. "I never thought Jack would break up with her."

"Neither did she," Bill said drowsily.

"I hope she'll be okay," I said. "Do you think she'll be okay?"

"Yep," Bill murmured.

"A broken engagement, a car crash, a mysterious stranger, and a secret chapel . . ." A snort of laughter escaped me. "The Handmaidens will spit tacks when they find out what they missed."

"Mmm-hmm," Bill mumbled.

Grinning into the darkness, I rolled onto my side and slid gently into a deep, dreamless sleep. Had I known where the evening's events would lead, I would have lain awake until dawn.

Seven

Since Bess rose with the larks on Sunday morning, Bill and I rose with them, too, but we were layabouts compared with our fellow house guests. We arrived in the bacon-scented kitchen to find Emma loading the dishwasher on her own, but only because everyone else was out and about, not only awake but active.

"Kit, Nell, Cassie, and your sons are in the stables," she informed us. "Derek, Peter, Mr. Barlow, and Bree are spreading a mixture of sand and straw on the lane. Charles and Grant are restoring order to the great hall, bless them, and Tilly's in the chapel with Lilian and the vicar." She smiled wryly. "I'm not used to having a clandestine chapel on the premises. I still think of it as a storage room."

"Was Lilian furious with us for not waking her last night?" I asked.

"Quite the opposite," Emma replied. "She claims she would have been furious if we'd dragged her out of bed."

"Good call," I acknowledged.

To judge by the number of egg-stained dishes Emma was handling, many breakfasts had already been eaten. I passed Bess to Bill and stepped up to the stove to make ours. Bess immediately squirmed out of her father's arms to conduct a thorough examination of the kitchen's lower reaches. Bill shadowed her to keep her from ransacking the cabinets.

"Who should we thank for bringing the high chair to the kitchen?" he asked.

"Derek," Emma answered. "He loves having a little one in the house. He's wanted to be a grandfather ever since he became a father."

"Granddad Derek," I said. "It has a nice ring to it. How's Tilly doing?"

"As far as I can tell, she's fine," said Emma. "Unfortunately, her car isn't."

"Can Mr. Barlow repair it?" Bill asked.

"He thinks so, but it may take a while." Emma hit the switch on the dishwasher and seated herself at the table with a groan that suggested she'd been on her feet for too long. "I invited Tilly to stay with us until her car is ready, but she's dithering."

"Why?" I asked. "Would she rather spend Christmas by herself in a hotel in Tewkesbury?"

"I don't think so," said Emma, "but she's reluctant to be a burden—her word, not mine."

"Tell her you owe her a month's room and board for identifying the chapel," Bill suggested.

"Great idea," said Emma. "I'll try it. I'm going to invite Bree to stay with us, too."

"I was going to invite her to stay with us," I protested.

"There may be a bidding war," Lilian warned as she, the vicar, Tilly, Grant, and Charles entered the kitchen. "None of us like the thought of leaving the poor girl alone in that big house of hers at Christmastime."

"It's unthinkable," said the vicar. "She can have her choice of guest rooms at the vicarage."

"We may have only one guest room," said Charles, "but it's beautifully decorated."

"See what I mean?" said Lilian. "A bidding war."

"Pop Bess in her chair, Bill," I said. "Our breakfast is ready."

"Is there any more tea in the pot?" Grant inquired.

"I could do with another slice of toast," said Charles.

"I could do with another breakfast," Peter declared.

Peter's sentiment was echoed by the rest of the stable crew as they streamed into the kitchen, and by the road crew, who followed close upon their heels. Rob and Will looked none the worse for wear after their night in the hayloft. Like the others, they were rosy-cheeked, bright-eyed, and, evidently, famished. Emma, by contrast, looked as though she wanted nothing more than to go back to bed.

Charles must have noticed her expression, because he planted his hands on her shoulders, saying, "Do not stir, good lady. We will shift for ourselves."

And shift they did, setting the table, raiding the refrigerator, and falling upon the leftover leftovers like a pack of ravenous wolves. Tilly, Lilian, and the vicar were more decorous, but they, too, filled their plates while Bill, Bess, and I continued to work our way through modest portions of scrambled eggs and thick slices of buttered toast. I'd felt that a light meal was in order after the previous evening's indulgences, but mine was clearly a minority opinion.

"Have you been introduced to everyone, Tilly?" the vicar asked.

"Not quite," she replied, turning to look at Bill and me.

"I'm Lori Shepherd," I said.

"I'm Lori's husband, Bill Willis," said Bill. "The twins are our sons, Will and Rob, and the little girl with egg on her face is our daughter, Bess."

"I Bess," said Bess through a mouthful of toast.

"You're adorable, Bess," said Tilly. "I'm very pleased to meet you."

Tilly was more neatly attired than those of us who hadn't had the foresight to bring a change of clothes with us to the party. She was, however, dressed as somberly as she had been when she'd arrived at Anscombe Manor, though the jet brooch pinned to her black cardigan was scarcely visible.

I cocked my head toward the brooch and shot an inquiring look across the table at Lilian. She indicated with a minute shrug that she'd been unable to discover whether our new acquaintance was in mourning or whether she was merely partial to Victorian jewelry.

While Lilian and I conducted our mute dialogue, my husband interrogated Derek about the road conditions.

"Is the lane still frozen?" he asked.

"It's slick," Derek allowed, "but we've made it navigable. If you take it easy, you'll be able to drive home without—" He broke off and glanced apologetically at Tilly, who finished the sentence for him.

"Without ending up in a ditch," she said, blushing furiously. "So stupid of me."

"Nothing stupid about it," said Mr. Barlow. "It's tricky to drive on ice."

"Just ask Lori," Bill put in.

"I slid into a ditch once, *a long time ago*," I said, kicking him under the table. "It's the sort of thing that could happen to anyone."

"The ice should be gone by noon in any case," Emma interjected. "According to the weather report, a warm-up is on the way."

"Ice or no ice," said Mr. Barlow, "you won't be going anywhere soon, Miss Trout. Derek towed your car to my workshop and I took a closer look at it. You were right about the struts—they're busted. Fact is, they were hanging on by the turn of a screw. It's just as well they broke when they did. At speed . . ." He shook his head. "Would've been catastrophic."

"But it wasn't," I said quickly as the color drained from Tilly's face. "You're safe and sound, Tilly."

"It seems as if I'm lucky, too," she said faintly.

"You are," said Mr. Barlow. "Old cars need proper maintenance, Miss Trout, but don't worry. Bree and I will make sure your vehicle is up to snuff before you get behind the wheel again."

"Are you a mechanic, Bree?" Tilly asked.

"Bree's my apprentice," Mr. Barlow said proudly. "Don't know what I'd do without her."

Bree, who hadn't spoken since she'd entered the kitchen, glanced gratefully at Mr. Barlow, then continued to stare bleakly at the untouched food on her plate.

"How wonderful," said Tilly. "I envy you, Bree."

"Do you?" Bree said wanly. "I don't know why you would."

Though it was clear to me that Bree was thinking of her unenviable position as a jilted fiancée, it evidently wasn't clear to Tilly.

"I envy you because you have so many avenues open to you," Tilly explained. "Women worked as motor mechanics during the war, of course, but they lost their jobs as soon as the men came home. When I was a girl, I wasn't given the option of learning how to repair cars. You're fortunate to be able to do as you please."

"I suppose so," said Bree, and while she didn't seize her fork and begin to shovel reheated potatoes into her mouth, she sat up a bit straighter and nibbled on a sliver of cold turkey.

I longed to give Tilly a pat on the back for reminding Bree that there was more to life than marriage, but I didn't want to startle her, so I restrained myself. Meanwhile, Derek took the conversation in a completely different direction.

"Well?" he said, looking from Lilian to the vicar. "What do you think of our chapel?"

"I think it's a treasure," said Lilian. "At the same time, I can't help seeing it as a sad reminder of England's long history of religious intolerance."

"It's both a treasure and a sad reminder," said the vicar, "but I doubt that it's unique. There must be other disguised chapels in other English homes waiting for a keen-eyed scholar to recognize them."

Tilly didn't seem to realize that he'd paid her an oblique compliment, but she proved that she deserved it by contributing to the discussion with the enthusiasm of a keen-eyed scholar.

"Some are quite easily identified," she said. "The Bar Convent chapel in York has a neoclassical domed sanctuary, a nave with three bays, a north and south transept, and a Lady Chapel. It's quite large and it's unmistakably Roman Catholic, yet it was kept hidden from unfriendly eyes for more than a hundred years."

"Fascinating," I said. "Are you a historian?"

Tilly shook her head, saying modestly, "I would never lay claim to such an exalted title."

"Are you a librarian?" asked Grant.

"I'm afraid not," said Tilly.

"You know a lot about York," Charles pointed out. "Did you live there before you moved to Oxford?"

"I-I've always lived in Oxford," Tilly stammered, sounding flustered. "I've never even visited York."

"Then why—" I began, but Mr. Barlow cut me off.

"Let her alone, will you?" he scolded. "I know what a nosy lot you are, but she doesn't. It's too early in the day to be poking and prying into her personal life."

"Sorry, Tilly," I said.

"Sorry," said Grant.

"Apologies," said Charles.

"Not at all," Tilly murmured, her gaze fixed on her teacup.

Bill ended the awkward pause that followed by asking, "Will you hold the morning service in the chapel, Vicar?"

"I will not," the vicar stated firmly. "It would be highly disrespectful to hold an Anglican service in a Roman Catholic chapel. If no one objects, we can hold the service here, in the kitchen. Our Lord won't mind."

"For where two or three are gathered together in my name," Lilian recited, "I am in the midst of them."

"Matthew," Tilly said half to herself, "chapter eighteen, verse twenty."

"Quite right," said the vicar. "We'll finish eating first, of course."

After the table was cleared, the vicar said a heartfelt and quite lengthy prayer of thanksgiving for, among many other things, family, friends, food, drink, the queen, the queen's family, and the safe deliverance of Miss Matilda Trout. Tilly blinked confusedly when the vicar mentioned her by name, but by the time he gave the final blessing, she'd regained her composure.

After the blessing, Lilian slipped her arm into her husband's, saying, "Let us now give Emma and Derek a chance to recover from the rigors of their delightful Christmas party."

"Not before we give them three cheers," said Charles.

Will, Rob, and Bess led the rest of us in the rousing chorus of "hip, hip, hoorahs" that brought the party to its delayed conclusion. I lifted Bess from the high chair, wiped her down, and carried her to the cloakroom. Bill herded the boys in the same direction, and in less than twenty minutes, we were on our way home.

While Will and Rob entertained us with a detailed account of their night in the stables, which involved sweeping stalls, cleaning curry combs, and spying a rat among the hay bales after the barn cat had forsaken his duties and curled up in Rob's sleeping bag, I took in the beauty the storm had left in its wake. Tiny icicles hung from the hedgerows, the pastures gleamed like frozen ponds, and our cottage, with Stanley peering at us through the lacy frost on the living room's bay window, would not have looked out of place on a Christmas card.

Bill topped up Stanley's water bowls as soon as we reached the kitchen, and I deposited an entire can of tuna in his food bowl to make amends for our prolonged absence. We showered him with affection as well, but he was much more interested in the tuna.

Since I'd already dressed Bess in the spare clothes I'd brought with me to Anscombe Manor, she didn't look as ratty as the rest of us. I sent the boys upstairs to change into jeans and flannel shirts that weren't covered with wisps of hay, while Bill and I took turns putting on fresh clothing and keeping an eye on our dangerously mobile daughter.

Bill would have gladly settled down for a nap in his favorite armchair, but the boys corralled him into taking a walk through the oak grove that stretched from our cottage all the way to Anscombe Manor. Bess, who'd gotten a lot more sleep than we had, was eager to join the expedition, so Bill bundled her up and pulled her behind him on a sled. I waved them off from the back garden, then retreated hurriedly to the cottage.

I wasn't sure how much time I would have before my loved ones returned, demanding hot chocolate and the oatmeal cookies I'd baked earlier in the week, but I intended to put every minute of it to good use. While Bill, Bess, and the boys explored the frozen forest, I'd be in the study, sharing a bumper crop of gossip with Aunt Dimity.

Eight

Hardly a day went by when I didn't speak with Aunt Dimity. I seldom spoke of her, however, because she and I had a somewhat unusual relationship. For one thing, Aunt Dimity wasn't my aunt. For another, she wasn't, strictly speaking, alive. The former was easier to explain than the latter.

Dimity Westwood, an Englishwoman born and bred, had been my late mother's closest friend. The pair had met in London while serving their respective countries during the Second World War. The hardships they shared during those dark and dangerous years forged a bond of affection between them that was never broken.

When the war in Europe ended and my mother sailed back to the States, she and Dimity maintained their friendship by sending hundreds of letters back and forth across the Atlantic. After my father's sudden death, those letters became my mother's refuge, a tranquil haven in which she could find respite from the everyday challenges of teaching full time while raising a rambunctious daughter on her own.

My mother was fiercely protective of her refuge. She told no one about it, not even her only child. When I was growing up, I knew Dimity Westwood only as Aunt Dimity, the redoubtable heroine of a series of bedtime stories invented by my mother. I had no idea that my favorite fictional character was a real woman until after both she and my mother had died.

It was then that Dimity Westwood bequeathed to me a comfortable fortune, the honey-colored cottage that had been her childhood home, the precious postwar correspondence she'd exchanged with my mother, and a curious book filled with blank pages and bound in blue leather. It was through the blue journal that I finally came to know my benefactress.

Whenever I opened the journal, Aunt Dimity's handwriting would appear, an old-fashioned copperplate taught in the village school at a time when a computer was a person who used pen and paper to perform complex calculations. I nearly jumped out of my skin the first time it happened, but I quickly realized that Aunt Dimity's intentions were wholly benevolent.

I couldn't explain how Aunt Dimity managed to bridge the gap between life and afterlife—and she wasn't too clear about it either—but I didn't require a technical explanation. The important bit, the only bit that mattered to me, was that she was as good a friend to me as she'd been to my mother.

The study was still, silent, and nearly as dark as a cave when I entered it. Frozen droplets dangled like earrings from the strands of ivy that crisscrossed the diamond-paned windows above the old oak desk, but they did little to dispel the gloom of yet another overcast day. I hastened to switch on the mantel shelf lamps, then knelt to light a fire in the hearth. As soon as the flames began to dance, I stood to greet my oldest friend in the world.

"Hi, Reginald," I said. "Did you miss us?"

Reginald was a small, powder-pink flannel rabbit with black button eyes and beautifully hand-sewn whiskers. My mother had placed him in my bassinet shortly after my birth, and he'd been by my side ever since. A sensible woman would have put him away when she put away childish things, but I wasn't a sensible woman. My pink bunny sat in a special niche in the study's tall bookshelves, where I could see him and chat with him and let him know that he was not forgotten.

"We were waylaid by an ice storm," I told him. "You'll hear all about it if you listen in."

The gleam in Reginald's black button eyes told me that he would, *of course*, eavesdrop on my conversation with Aunt Dimity. He was as interested in local news as I was.

I gave his pink ears an affectionate twiddle, then took the blue journal from its shelf and carried it with me to one of the tall leather armchairs facing the hearth. While the fire crackled and snapped, I curled up in the armchair, cradled the journal in one hand, and opened it.

"Dimity?" I said. "I've got so much to tell you that I hardly know where to begin."

I sat back, propped my feet on the ottoman, and smiled as the familiar handwriting began to curl and loop gracefully across the blank page.

Good morning, Lori. You sound very excited. Did something thrilling happen at Emma's party?

"Quite a few thrilling things happened," I replied. "I would have told you about them last night, but we were stranded at Anscombe Manor by an ice storm."

Marooned by disagreeable weather again, my dear? I hope you didn't have to sleep in an attic this time.

"I didn't," I assured her. "Bill, Bess, and I shared a comfortable bedroom on the ground floor."

I'm glad to hear it. Attics have their uses, but as you discovered when the flood stranded you in East Sussex, they tend to be rather cluttered and extremely dusty. Would I be correct in assuming that Will and Rob slept in the stables?

"Where else?" I said, grinning. "Believe it or not, the ice storm wasn't the biggest news of the night."

What was?

"It's tough to choose," I said, "but I'd have to go with Bree's shocking announcement."

Shocking announcements usually top the list of thrilling events at a party.

"Bree's definitely comes in at number one," I confirmed. "I hate to be the bearer of bad news, Dimity, but the engagement's off."

Oh, dear. Has Bree fallen out of love with Jack MacBride?

"Other way round," I said. "Jack's fallen out of love with Bree. He called her from Stockholm yesterday morning to end their engagement."

He broke up with her over the telephone?

"Pretty cowardly, huh?" I said.

Jack never struck me as cowardly. Perhaps he was stranded in Stockholm by the same weather system that stranded you. Since he couldn't fly to England to speak with Bree face-to-face, and since he felt compelled to be honest with her, he had no choice but to deliver the sad tidings over the telephone.

"You're much kinder than I am," I said. "Your scenario may even be true, but it hardly matters because the message is the same either way: Jack broke up with Bree because he's fallen for a Swedish microbiologist who likes to travel."

Perhaps it's for the best. Bree has become something of a homebody since she inherited her great-grandaunts' house, and Jack's conservation work takes him all over the world. He may be better off with a partner who enjoys living out of a suitcase.

"And Bree may be better off with someone other than Jack," I said, "but right now she looks crushed."

Few things in life are more melancholy than a broken heart at Christmastime. I hope you'll do your best to help her to bounce back from the blow.

"You know I will," I said. "We all will. Charles and Grant are going to throw a pity party for her after the holidays, and Mr. Barlow asked her to work on Tilly's car with him."

Charles and Grant throw splendid parties, but I suspect that Mr. Barlow's cure will be more efficacious in the long run.

"So do I," I said. "It'll keep her from sitting at home, feeling sorry for herself."

True, but there's more to it than that. Mr. Barlow is exactly the sort of company Bree needs at the moment. He won't tiptoe around her or pummel her with questions about her feelings.

"As I would?" I said ruefully.

Not just you, my dear. Most of her friends will be too solicitous or too intrusive. Either response will serve only to make Bree more self-conscious than she already is.

"I can guarantee that Mr. Barlow won't ask her to share her feelings," I said decisively. "He'd sooner dance naked on the village green."

Either activity would be anathema to him. Instead of prying into Bree's personal life, Mr. Barlow will simply get on with the job at hand and he'll rely upon her to get on with it, too. By doing so, he'll remind her of her capabilities rather than her loss. Bree enjoys being useful, and doing something for someone else is the surest way to recover from a setback. By repairing the car, Bree will be helping Mr. Barlow as well as Tilly. Which leads me to my next line of inquiry: Who, may I ask, is Tilly? And what happened to her car?

"Tilly is Matilda Trout—*Miss* Matilda Trout—a middle-aged woman who lives in Oxford," I explained. "She was on her way to a hotel in Tewkesbury when she got lost in the fog. When she saw the manor lit up like a Christmas tree, she turned into the drive to ask for directions, slid on the ice, and crashed into a drainage ditch."

Good heavens! Is she all right?

"She's fine," I said, "but she won't be able to drive her car until Mr. Barlow and Bree fix it. Emma's made it crystal clear to her that she's welcome to stay at the manor while her car is under repair."

I'm sure Emma means well, but if I were Tilly, I'd prefer to be driven home by a friend or a family member.

"I don't think Tilly has a friend or a family member," I said. "She was driving to Tewkesbury by herself, Dimity, and when Emma offered to call someone for her after the accident, she said there was no one to call."

It sounds as though she intended to spend Christmas on her own at the hotel in Tewkesbury.

"It does," I said, "but Lilian Bunting and I doubt that Tilly's alone by choice."

What do you mean?

"Tilly dresses almost entirely in black, as if she's in mourning," I said. "She even wears a jet mourning brooch. Lilian and I think someone close to her died recently."

If so, the poor woman's head must be spinning. To have her holiday plans overthrown by an accident while she's still in the midst of grieving for a lost loved one—she must feel overwhelmed by misfortune. Could her employer, perhaps, come and fetch her?

"She didn't mention having an employer or a job," I said. "I don't know what Tilly does for a living, Dimity, but she seems to have a working knowledge of car mechanics and a thorough knowledge of the persecution of Roman Catholics in sixteenth-century England. And before you ask, she denied being a historian or a librarian."

I can understand why the subject of motor mechanics would come up in the course of the evening—it stands to reason that Tilly would be concerned about her car—but how on earth did she work Anglo-Catholic persecution into the conversation?

"Blame it on Emma," I said. "She asked us to look at a peculiar room in the manor. None of us could figure out why it had been built or what purpose it served, but Tilly knew what it was five minutes after she walked into it. She wasn't reacting to a gut feeling, either. She interpreted physical evidence we'd overlooked, even though it was right in front of our faces."

Will you tell me what the room is, or would you like me to guess?

"I'll tell you," I said, and continued hastily. "Tilly identified the room as a clandestine chapel where Roman Catholics worshiped in secret to avoid persecution. Were you aware of the manor's secret chapel?"

I was not. To my knowledge, the Anscombes have always been practicing Anglicans.

"But the Anscombes haven't always owned the manor," I pointed out. "In Tudor times, it was owned by the Mandeville family. The part of the house containing the chapel was built during their tenure."

I begin to follow Tilly's argument. "Mandeville" could very well be a Norman name. If the Mandevilles were an old Norman family, they might not have accepted Henry VIII's religious reforms.

"Emma can't find records to confirm it," I said, "but Tilly believes the Mandevilles created the chapel for their own personal use. She also thinks the Crown may have confiscated Anscombe Manor from the Roman Catholic Mandevilles and sold it to the Protestant Anscombes."

If the Anscombes realized that the room was a Roman Catholic chapel, they wouldn't have broadcast its presence in their home.

"They didn't even label the room as a chapel on the house plans Emma found," I said. "On the plans, it's just a room."

I never fail to be amazed by the layers of history hidden within very old buildings. Emma and Derek must be grateful to Tilly for unveiling one of the manor's best-kept secrets. Is there a priest hole in the chapel?

"A what?" I said.

A priest hole. Surely Tilly searched for a priest hole. Its presence would confirm her claim beyond all reasonable doubt.

"She didn't say anything about a priest hole," I said. "What's a priest hole?

A priest hole, sometimes called a priest closet, was a hiding place for priests as well as for the paraphernalia associated with the Roman Catholic mass—vestments or a crucifix, for example. During Elizabeth I's reign, priests were looked upon as heretics and spies. If a priest was discovered celebrating the sacraments anywhere in England, he could be found guilty of high treason and executed, sometimes after a prolonged period of gruesome torture. It was essential, therefore, to conceal priests from the prying eyes of the Crown's pursuivants, or priest hunters. Hence, the construction of priest holes.

"You seem to know an awful lot about priest holes," I said.

I became interested in them after I visited Scotney Castle in Kent. In Elizabethan times, a Jesuit priest named Richard Blount managed to live undetected at Scotney Castle for seven years, thanks to a priest hole hidden in a wall cupboard in a back staircase. He didn't live in the priest hole, of course, but it was there when he needed it.

"What does a priest hole look like?" I asked. "Are they always hidden in wall cupboards?"

They could be hidden almost anywhere. The usual procedure was to create a concealed cavity beneath floorboards, under a stairway, or within a wall. The cavity would then be fitted with a disguised door or hatch that could be swiftly opened and shut. If a priest hunter approached the house, the priest could slip into the priest hole with the telltale paraphernalia and hide there until the coast was clear, or until he was discovered and dragged from his hiding place to his doom.

"The good old days, eh?" I said with a derisive snort.

Let us learn from them the value of religious tolerance. I wonder . . .

"What do you wonder?" I asked.

I wonder if Tilly is, or was, a nun. It would explain her plain attire, her solitude, and her in-depth knowledge of Anglo-Catholic history. It would not, however, explain her failure to search the chapel for a priest hole.

"It was very late, Dimity," I said, "and, as you pointed out, her head must have been spinning. I'll ask her about priest holes the next time I see her—if there is a next time. I really hope Emma persuades her to stay at the manor. Whether Tilly's a runaway nun or not, she's someone I'd like to know better."

She also appears to be someone who is in dire need of friends.

"In which case, she'd be a fool to turn down Emma's invitation," I said. "She'll find nothing *but* friends at Anscombe Manor."

So she will. My goodness, Lori, you did have a memorable evening, though I imagine Emma would have preferred it to be memorable for reasons other than a broken engagement and an automobile accident. On a much lighter note: Were your tartlets a success?

"They were," I replied proudly. "The only snacks more popular than my tartlets were some Indian sweets Emma made, and even then it was neck and neck. I could have made twice as many tartlets and they would have disappeared in a twinkling, though I wouldn't have been able to transport them because I don't have enough——" I interrupted myself with a groan.

What's wrong?

"I'm such an idiot, Dimity," I said, shaking my head. "I left my storage containers in Emma's kitchen."

Look upon it as an opportunity, my dear. When you pick them up, you can mount a search for the priest hole in the chapel. Do I hear shouting in the distance?

"You do," I said, cocking an ear toward the study door. "Gotta go, Dimity. The arctic explorers are demanding hot chocolate."

With marshmallows, I trust!

I laughed, and when the curving lines of royal-blue ink had faded from the page, I closed the journal and returned it to its shelf. I paused to touch a finger to Reginald's pink flannel snout, then headed for the kitchen to dig a bag of marshmallows out of the pantry and to ask Bill if he would mind looking after the children for another hour or so. I had a sudden hankering to do a little exploring of my own.

Nine

Invigorated by his walk, Bill agreed to postpone his nap until I returned from Anscombe Manor, though he doubted that I'd be home in time for lunch.

"Knowing you as I do," he said, "I won't be shocked if you're gone for the rest of the day, or possibly for the next month, but don't hurry back on my account. I can make lunch *and* dinner, if need be."

"Of course you can," I said. "Your talents know no bounds." I gave him a quick kiss. "But I promise to be home in time for dinner."

Will, Rob, and Bess were guzzling hot chocolate and munching on oatmeal cookies at the kitchen table while they sorted through the rocks, twigs, acorns, leaves, seedpods, and interesting weeds they'd brought back from the oak grove.

"Everything's dripping, Mum," said Will, "so the lane should be okay."

"Good to know," I said. "Be nice to your father while I'm gone. He didn't get much sleep last night."

"Should've slept in the hayloft with us," Rob mumbled through a mouthful of cookie.

"Hay!" Bess agreed.

I planted a kiss on her head, grabbed my jacket and my shoulder bag from the hatstand in the front hall, and took off for

Anscombe Manor. Since the Range Rover was equipped with child safety seats, I left it in the driveway and used Bill's car instead. His Mercedes handled beautifully, but it hardly mattered, because the warm-up was well under way. Droplets fell like rain from the melting icicles on the hedgerows and flowed in braided streams across the narrow, twisting lane. Instead of creeping cautiously over straw-strewn ice, I splashed fearlessly through puddles littered with floating straw.

Mr. Barlow's car was the only vehicle parked on the graveled apron when I arrived at Anscombe Manor. I pulled in next to his aged sedan and, as the front entrance was used principally for special occasions, I made my way to the back of the manor house, to let myself in through the kitchen door.

I ran into Kit in the cobbled courtyard behind the manor. He informed me that Nell was exercising a horse in the enclosed arena while Derek and Peter worked on the day nursery under Cassie's supervision.

"Cassie would rather swing a hammer," he said, "but Peter won't allow her to exert herself."

"I should think not," I said. "We don't want the baby to pop out before the nursery's finished. If I were Cassie, I'd take it easy until the baby's born. She won't get much rest afterward."

"So I've heard," said Kit, smiling. "You'll find Emma, Tilly, and Mr. Barlow in the kitchen."

"I noticed Mr. Barlow's car out front," I said. "Why isn't he in his workshop with Bree, repairing Tilly's car?"

"You'll have to ask him," said Kit, "though he may not give you a truthful answer."

"Why?" I said lightly. "Is he hiding a deep, dark secret?"

"In a manner of speaking." Kit scanned the courtyard, as if to make certain that we were alone, before he replied, "Nell thinks Mr. Barlow has fallen head over heels for Tilly."

"Does she?" I paused to review Mr. Barlow's behavior since Tilly's car had landed in the drainage ditch, then nodded slowly. "Nell may be right, Kit."

"Nell's never wrong about affairs of the heart," he said.

I couldn't argue with him. Nell had always had an uncanny insight into the workings of the human heart. She'd been all of five years old when she'd predicted Emma's marriage to Derek, and she'd been aware of Kit's feelings for her long before he'd admitted them to himself.

"I don't know how I missed it," I said. "Mr. Barlow has been acting like a grouchy knight in shining armor ever since he rescued Tilly. He scolded us for staring at her in the great hall last night, and he nearly bit our heads off when we asked her a few simple questions this morning."

"Tread carefully," Kit advised. "You don't want to get on the wrong side of a grouchy knight."

"Thanks for the warning," I said. "I won't pummel Tilly with questions—until Mr. Barlow leaves."

Kit laughed and strode across the courtyard to the stables. I opened the kitchen door and stepped inside to find Mr. Barlow seated across the kitchen table from Emma, who looked as if her patience was wearing thin, and Tilly, who looked distressed. Tilly was dressed in yet another drab ensemble—black skirt, gray blouse, and black cardigan, with the jet brooch pinned at her breast.

"Morning, all," I said. "Sorry to barge in, but I left my storage containers behind." I studied Tilly's tragic countenance for a moment, then asked, "Is everything okay?"

"No," she said, staring at her tightly folded hands. "Mr. Barlow very kindly came to break the bad news to me in person."

Jack MacBride could learn a lesson or two from our grouchy knight, I thought, but aloud I said, "What bad news?"

"No one's died, though you couldn't tell it by the way Miss Trout's carrying on," Mr. Barlow said, rolling his eyes. "I just need to order parts, is all."

"It won't be easy to obtain replacement parts for such an old vehicle during the holidays," Tilly said woefully. "It could take a fortnight, perhaps longer. I couldn't possibly trespass on Emma's hospitality for an entire fortnight. There must be a hotel nearby."

"There are several hotels in Upper Deeping," I said, "and all of them will be booked solid."

Emma gazed imploringly at me. "Please tell Tilly that I mean it when I say she's welcome to stay with us."

"Emma doesn't say things she doesn't mean," I said. "You can see for yourself that she has enough room to house an army, and she could feed one, too, with plenty of food to spare." I sat beside Mr. Barlow, rested my elbows on the table, and continued, "If you want to go home, I'll drive you, but if you want to do Emma an enormous favor, you'll stay here."

"A favor?" said Tilly, lifting her lowered eyes to look doubtfully at me. "What sort of favor could *I* do for Emma?"

"You could search the house archives for references to the chapel," I said.

"Oh, *yes*," said Emma, with an enthusiasm born of relief. "I'd *love* to know more about the chapel, but I never seem to find the time to comb through the archives. I'd be *incredibly* grateful to you if you'd do it for me, Tilly."

"Well," Tilly said hesitantly, "if I could be of service . . ."

"You'd be of *tremendous* service," Emma assured her.

"Then I'll be glad to accept your invitation," said Tilly.

Mr. Barlow stood. "Now that you've come to your senses, I'll get back to work. Bree should have delivered your food parcels by now, Emma. She can help me take the tires off the Peugeot." He moved toward the door, hesitated, and swung around to face Tilly again. "If you need a break from the archives, Miss Trout, I could show you around our church."

"Thank you," said Tilly, "but I wouldn't dream of——"

"Yes, you would," Emma broke in. "You'll think more clearly if you take a break now and again."

Tilly seemed to weigh the suggestion carefully. "I'm not accustomed to taking breaks, but if you advise it——"

"I do," Emma said adamantly.

"May I ring you?" Tilly asked Mr. Barlow.

"Yes," he said, his voice cracking like a teenager's. He cleared his throat and repeated more forcefully, "Yes. Emma has my number. Ring anytime and I'll come and fetch you. Good day, ladies."

He let himself out through the kitchen door, though it took him two tries to lift the latch far enough to open the door. Nell's never wrong about affairs of the heart, I reminded myself as I watched him fumble with a latch he'd lifted a hundred times before. Mr. Barlow is in love with Tilly Trout.

"We keep the house archives in the library," Emma was saying to Tilly. "I can take you there now, if you like."

"Hold on," I said. "Before you dive into the archives, Tilly, there's another subject I'd like to discuss with you. I was thinking about Scotney Castle after I got home this morning, and—"

"Why were you thinking about Scotney Castle?" Emma interrupted. "Are you planning a visit?"

Emma was one of the handful of people who knew about my disembodied houseguest. If she and I had been alone, I wouldn't have hesitated to tell her about my conversation with Aunt Dimity. I did not, however, intend to inform Tilly that I'd spent the morning chatting with a dead woman.

"I'm not planning a visit," I said. "It's just one of those things that drifted into my mind." I gave Emma a repressive look before turning to Tilly. "It struck me that, if Scotney Castle has a priest hole, Emma's chapel might have one, too. Why didn't you look for a priest hole when you were in the chapel last night?"

Tilly blinked at me dumbly, then shook her head, looking chagrined. "I hope you'll forgive me, Emma. I must have been overtired, because it simply never occurred to me to look for a priest hole."

"I'll forgive you," said Emma, "if you'll tell me what a priest hole is."

"Tell her on the way to the chapel," I recommended, getting to my feet. "Come on, you two. We'll search for the priest hole together."

"We'll need torches," said Tilly. "And brooms."

"Brooms?" I queried.

"The handles will be useful for floor tapping," Tilly explained.

Equipped with the tools of the priest-hole hunter's trade, we strode purposefully to the chapel. As she had the previous evening, Tilly shed her shyness as soon as she was asked to share her knowledge. While we walked, she delivered a lecture on priest holes that put Aunt Dimity's in the shade. I was particularly appalled by the tale of Nicholas Owen, the Jesuit lay brother responsible for the construction of numerous priest holes during the reigns of Elizabeth I and James I.

"Brother Nicholas was lame and quite tiny," Tilly informed us, "yet he always worked alone, sometimes in the dead of night, cutting through stonework or thick oak floorboards to create his hiding places."

"He must have been a prime target for the priest hunters," I said.

"Indeed, he was," Tilly concurred. "He evaded them until 1606, when he was captured, conveyed to the Tower of London, and tortured to death on the rack. Despite suffering untold agonies, he never imparted a scintilla of useful information to his captors."

"A brave man," I murmured hollowly, trying not to imagine his untold agonies.

"Brother Nicholas was canonized in 1970," Tilly said brightly, as if sainthood made his horrific death less dreadful. "I think he'd be pleased to know that he's the patron saint of illusionists and escapologists, don't you?"

"I'm sure he would," I said, exchanging aghast grimaces with Emma behind Tilly's back. "I don't think I've ever met anyone who knows as much as you do about the history of the Roman Catholic Church in England. You wouldn't happen to be a nun, would you?"

"I attend church regularly," she replied seriously, "but I've never felt the call to take Holy Orders. I'm nothing more than a lay member of the Church of England." She clasped her hands together.

"Wouldn't it be wonderful if we discovered one of Brother Nicholas's priest holes in your chapel, Emma?"

"How would we know it was one of his?" Emma asked. "He didn't sign them, did he?"

"No, but certain features have come to be associated with his work," said Tilly. "Brother Nicholas was known for creating double-blind priest holes—hiding places that contained two compartments, one in front of or below the other. Upon finding the first compartment empty, the priest hunters would conclude their search, leaving the priest safe and sound in the second compartment."

"How thick are the chapel walls?" I asked Emma.

"The exterior wall is three feet thick, and it's made of stone blocks," she replied. "Derek measured it a few years ago. We used to joke that the original builders aimed for a castle and ended up with a manor house, but now I'm not so sure."

"A three-foot-thick wall would be roomy enough for a priest hole," I pointed out.

"It suggests to me that the builder included a priest hole in his plan for the chapel," said Tilly. "An unusual occurrence, but not entirely without precedent."

Before Tilly could offer us a list of historic houses with similar architectural features, Emma opened the chapel door and turned on the wall sconces.

"Where do we begin?" she asked.

"With the floor, I think," said Tilly. She flipped her broom upside down and demonstrated the correct tapping technique. "If one of us hears a hollow sound, we'll stop to investigate."

We divided the floor into three zones, one for each of us, and walked slowly up and down the room, tapping our broom handles on the parquet. I wasn't sure I would recognize a "hollow sound" if I heard one, so I listened for any thump that stood out from the rest. None did, for me or for my companions. Though we tapped every square inch of the floor, we found nothing to investigate.

"The walls, then," said Tilly, undeterred.

"We don't have to tap them, do we?" said Emma. "I'd hate to dent the paneling."

"We'll look for hidden handles first," said Tilly. "Draw your fingers along the carved edges within each panel to feel for a notch or a bump—any feature that doesn't belong there."

Emma and I took a long wall apiece while Tilly concentrated on the short ones. It was slow going. The linenfold panels had so many edges that it took quite a while to slide our fingers along each of them. When Tilly finished examining the panels surrounding the door, she turned her attention to the panels at the end of the room where the disguised altar had once stood. Since we weren't listening for odd thumps anymore, she treated us to more fun facts about priest holes while she worked.

"The compartments were usually quite compact," she said. "It must have been exceedingly uncomfortable to sit or to crouch in a confined space, in total darkness, without making a noise for fear of alerting the priest hunters. Hunger and thirst could assail the hidden priest as well. A search could last for days in a house as large as Anscombe Manor."

"I'd rather face muscle cramps, hunger, and thirst than the rack," I said.

"So would I," said Emma.

"Naturally, one would," said Tilly. "Even so, it must have been terribly stressful to know that the slightest moan could mean the difference between life and . . . Oh!" she cried suddenly. "I've found it!"

She stood at the center of the altar wall, with one hand resting on a waist-high section of paneling that had swung wide to reveal a second, much plainer panel. Emma and I instantly abandoned our walls and rushed to the far end of the chapel to take a closer look at Tilly's find.

"There's a latch that opens it from the inside as well as the outside," she explained excitedly, indicating an inch-long piece of carving protruding from the bottom edge of the outer panel. "Imagine it opening silently after centuries of disuse," she marveled. "It quite takes my breath away."

"The inner panel would make the outer panel seem solid if a priest hunter tapped it," Emma said. "Ingenious."

"How do we open the inner panel?" I asked. "I don't see a handle."

"I believe it slides sideways," said Tilly.

"Slide it!" I urged.

"May I?" Tilly inquired, gazing hopefully at Emma.

When Emma nodded, Tilly wedged her fingertips into the seam at the left-hand edge of the inner panel. She tugged sideways and the panel slid open soundlessly to reveal a pitch-black cavity. While Emma and I gaped at the yawning hole in the stone wall behind the linenfold panel, Tilly staggered backward and covered her mouth with her hands.

"A priest hole," she whispered. "I've found a priest hole."

"Would you like to sit down, Tilly?" Emma asked, looking helplessly around the empty room. "I can bring a chair for you."

"No, no," said Tilly. "I'll be all right in a moment." She dropped her hands and took a steadying breath. "It's just a bit . . . overwhelming. I can't thank you enough for giving me the opportunity to make such a marvelous discovery."

"I should be thanking you," said Emma. "I didn't know what a priest hole was until you told me, so I wouldn't have searched for one. Are you a teacher?"

"A teacher!" Tilly exclaimed. She shook her head and said modestly, "I haven't the education to be a teacher."

"I beg to differ," said Emma. "You seem to be very well educated."

"You're very kind," said Tilly.

"We're all very thankful and kind and well educated," I said with a touch of asperity. "But now that we've found the priest hole, could we please take a look inside it?"

"Tilly first." Emma stepped aside and waved a hand toward the black cavity. "To the victor go the spoils."

"Are you quite sure?" Tilly asked.

"Discoverer's privilege," Emma stated firmly. "But remember to turn on your flashlight."

Tilly flicked the switch on her flashlight and thrust it before her as she poked her head inside the cavity.

"It's larger than I expected," she reported. "Ample headroom." She shone the light to her left, turned her head to follow the beam, and drew back from the cavity with a gasp.

"What is it, Tilly?" Emma asked. "What did you see?"

Tilly's eyes were like saucers as she replied in a breathless murmur, "Wonderful things!"

Ten

I hope you'll forgive me for paraphrasing Howard Carter's famous remark," Tilly went on, "but I can honestly say that I understand how he felt when he first peered into King Tutankhamen's tomb."

Since I'd expected her to say that she'd seen a rat, a bat, or the mummified remains of a long-forgotten Roman Catholic priest, I felt nothing but relief.

"Are you telling me there's a hoard of Egyptian treasures hidden in my wall?" Emma asked skeptically.

"Not Egyptian," said Tilly.

"I'm going in," I said impatiently.

I lit my flashlight, bent low, stepped through the opening, and straightened cautiously, though my caution proved to be unnecessary. Emma's priest hole was nothing like the cramped pockets Tilly had described. Instead, it resembled a long, narrow closet. Though Bill would have whacked his head on the ceiling, I could stand upright, and I could turn around easily, too. Chisel marks indicated that the stone wall had been hollowed out by a skilled mason who'd had the time to create fairly smooth surfaces by chipping off jagged edges.

The air within the priest hole was frigid, absolutely still, and filled with a scent I couldn't identify. It was musty, but not unpleasantly rank, so I doubted that it emanated from layers of guano or piles of rat droppings. I could easily imagine how dark it would be with the inner and outer panels shut. The thought of being trapped in impenetrable darkness for days on end sent a shiver down my spine, though the cold air may have been a contributing factor.

Emma's face appeared in the opening. "Well? What's it like?"

"Not too bad," I said. "I wouldn't want to use it as a vacation home, but on the whole—" I broke off with a gasp as I turned to my left. "Emma? You might want to get in here."

"Is there enough room?" Emma asked.

"Just get in here," I said, "and follow me. Tilly? You come, too."

I heard the two women enter the compartment behind me as I moved toward a sight that had already elicited gasps from both Tilly and me. I was fairly sure that it would make Emma gasp as well, but I was too preoccupied to pay attention to her initial reaction. The extraordinary tableau that had caught my eye seemed to be pulling me forward.

"What on earth . . . ?" said Emma as she shone her flashlight over my shoulder.

"It's not Egyptian," I said.

"It's not Christian, either," said Emma.

"I believe it's related to the Hindu religion," Tilly said helpfully, bringing up the rear.

"Strong possibility," I murmured, mesmerized.

I came to a halt before a plain oak bench draped with a square of silk cloth shot with gold thread and dyed in vibrant hues of red and yellow and green. A small bronze statue of a voluptuous goddess with four graceful arms and a benign smile stood atop the silk cloth. A tarnished brass incense burner and a shallow, tear-shaped brass bowl lay at the goddess's feet, surrounded by garlands of dried flowers and scattered handfuls of rubies and emeralds.

An elephant stood beside the statue, dwarfing it, but the elephant wasn't made of bronze. It was a soft toy decorated with gold braid, beaded tassels, tiny round mirrors, and brightly colored silk embroidery. As dazzling as the elephant was, however, it couldn't compete with the magnificent object lodged in the space between its tasseled trunk and its front legs.

The object was a golden heart overlaid with gold filigree, and it was as big as my fist. The bronze goddess gleamed and the gems glittered, but the gold heart shone like a star in the darkness as our flashlight beams converged on it.

"Oh, my," Tilly breathed.

"Uh-huh," I agreed dazedly.

"What is it?" Emma whispered. "A box?"

"Hard to tell," I whispered back. "I don't see a hinge, but the filigree could be concealing one."

We lapsed into stupefied silence until Emma came out of her trance.

"I'm getting cold," she declared in a determinedly everyday tone of voice, "and I can't think straight when I'm cold. Let's get out of here." She hesitated, then added, "Bring the heart, Lori."

I stretched my hand toward the golden heart, then looked over my shoulder and said with a guilty wince, "I feel like a grave robber, Emma."

"We're not in a grave and you're not a thief and I want to see the heart more clearly," Emma said crisply. "Bring it. But try not to disturb the garlands. The flowers look as though they'll turn to dust if you touch them." She paused. "They're marigolds, I think."

"Yes," Tilly said under her breath. "Marigolds."

"Turn around, Tilly," Emma said gently. "We're leaving."

As she and Tilly moved back toward the opening, I allowed my fingers to close around the heart. It was much heavier than I'd anticipated, so heavy that it nearly slipped from my grasp when I lifted it. I held it at eye level for a moment, wondering if it was made of solid gold. The thought of holding a fist-sized hunk of gold in the palm of my hand was so deeply unsettling that I told myself it was gold-plated lead.

"I'm sorry." I nodded respectfully to the goddess, but I spoke to the elephant, since the heart seemed to be his special treasure. "I'll try to bring it back to you when we're done with it, but the decision won't be mine to make. I promise you, we'll take good care of it. We're not looters."

"Come on, Lori!" Emma called from the opening. "You'll catch your death in there!"

"I probably will," I retorted, turning my back on the elephant. "You've heard of the curse of the pharaohs, haven't you?"

"Need I point out that you're not in Egypt?" Emma asked with a long-suffering sigh.

"I'm not sure where I am," I replied. As I emerged from the priest hole, the heart seemed to catch fire, glinting and gleaming majestically in the light from the wall sconces. "Could be Tudor England. Could be Tudor India." I held the heart out to Emma. "You tell me."

"I'm as mystified as you are," said Emma. Her gaze lingered on the heart, but she didn't take it from me. "Hang on to it for now, will you, Lori?"

"Why?" I said teasingly, waving the golden heart under her nose. "Afraid of the curse?"

"I'm afraid I'll drop a national treasure," she returned. "My hands are frozen." She tore her gaze away from the heart and smiled wryly as she closed the inner and outer panels. "Derek will kick himself when I show him the latch. He went over the paneling with a fine-tooth comb, looking for signs of dry rot and woodworm, but he missed the priest hole."

"Someone found it," I said. "Someone used it to conceal a secret that had nothing to do with persecuted priests. But who? And when? And what, exactly, was the secret?"

"I need a cup of tea," Emma said. "We *all* need a cup of tea. You must know the way to the kitchen by now, Tilly. Lead on!"

IF TILLY HAD led the way to the kitchen, we would have ended up in the attics. I was intrigued and perplexed by our discovery, but she seemed to be stunned by it. Emma had to put a guiding hand on her elbow to keep her from wandering aimlessly through the manor house.

Instead of delivering a learned talk on the curse of the pharaohs while we waited for the kettle to boil, Tilly remained tight-lipped and pensive. When I laid the heart before her on the kitchen table, she continued to stare into the middle distance, seemingly unaware of her surroundings. By mutual consent, Emma and I did nothing to derail her train of thought. We'd learned to respect her erudition.

We sat side by side across the table from Tilly and sipped our tea in silence while the cup Emma had prepared for her grew cold. We were halfway through our second cups before Tilly spoke.

"I've been thinking and thinking," she said, "but I cannot explain why someone would create a Hindu altar in a hiding place once used by Roman Catholic priests. There's not the least doubt that it *is* a Hindu altar, though it's a fairly rudimentary one. The bronze statue depicts Parvati, the Hindu goddess of fertility, love, and devotion. The elephant is an obvious reference to Parvati's son Ganesha, the elephant-headed god. Marigold garlands and incense are still used in Hindu ceremonies and celebrations."

I wasn't in the least surprised that Tilly would recognize the Hindu goddess of love or that she would be familiar with the goddess's elephant-headed son. She seemed to be a short, plump, human encyclopedia.

"The brass bowl on the altar," said Emma. "Is it used for holy water?"

"It's not a water bowl," Tilly informed her. "It's a *diya*—an oil lamp with a cotton wick that burns ghee, or clarified butter."

"I didn't see a wick or a buttery residue in the, er, *diya*," I said, stumbling over the unfamiliar word.

"There's no ash in the incense burner, either," Tilly pointed out. "Whoever created the altar must have decided that it would be unwise to kindle a flame in such an enclosed space."

"Extremely unwise," Emma agreed. "Smoke would fill the compartment in minutes, and I'd hate to think of what would happen if flames reached the oak panels."

"A conflagration would ensue," Tilly said. She tilted her head back to peer at the kitchen's vaulted ceiling. "The entire manor house could have burned to the ground."

"Which is why I'd hate to think of it," Emma muttered from the corner of her mouth.

I stifled a giggle and asked, "Could the rubies and emeralds be offerings, Tilly?"

"They could," she said, nodding, "but I don't know what to make of the heart." She lifted the dazzling artifact from the table and held it in one cupped hand while she studied it.

"I may be wrong," I said hesitantly, "but I think the heart may be made of solid gold."

"I'm quite certain it is," said Tilly.

Emma choked on a mouthful of tea. I patted her on the back while she wiped her chin with a napkin, but Tilly went on as if she hadn't noticed Emma's reaction to the news that we'd discovered a small—or, perhaps, a not-so-small—fortune in gold hidden in her wall.

"The heart is a superb example of Indian goldsmithing," Tilly continued, "but the initials puzzle me."

"Initials?" I said, frowning. "What initials?"

"They're woven into the filigree." Tilly lowered the heart to the table, then used an index finger to delineate a pair of letters all but hidden within the filigree's complex curvilinear pattern. "You see?" she said. "A *C* and an *M* are intertwined at the very center—dare I say, the heart?—of the applied decoration." She outlined the letters again, then released a dissatisfied sigh. "I don't understand why the goldsmith employed Roman letters rather than Sanskrit or one of the other elegant scripts associated with the Indian subcontinent."

"Can you read Sanskrit?" I asked out of sheer curiosity.

"No," Tilly replied regretfully. "I can get by in Latin and Greek, but I'm ashamed to say that I never learned Sanskrit."

"I can barely get by in English," I muttered. I expected Emma to giggle, but she didn't even crack a smile.

"Wait," she said, gazing intently at Tilly. "Back up a little, Tilly. Did you say that clarified butter is used in the brass lamp?"

"Ghee is used in the *diya*," Tilly corrected her. "But, yes, as the Hindu faith prohibits the use of tallow or any other animal fat as fuel, *diyas* are filled with clarified butter."

"Clarified butter," Emma repeated, looking thoughtful.

She got to her feet and crossed to a bookshelf in the corner of the kitchen. When she returned, she was holding a loosely bound, bulky volume that looked as if it might fall apart in her hands. She resumed her seat, placed the book on the table, and began to leaf through it gingerly. Each page appeared to contain a recipe written in the same tidy hand.

"I told you about my handwritten recipe book last night, Lori," she said.

"The one you found in the kitchen when you and Derek first moved into the manor," I said. "I remember."

"Then you'll also remember that I used a recipe from the book to make the sweets everyone liked," she said.

"The *Indian* sweets," I said, glancing at Tilly, who looked bemused.

"Here it is," said Emma. She removed a small sheet of yellowed paper that had been tucked into the book, laid it flat on the table, and tapped it with her finger. "The recipe for besan ladoo, an Indian sweet shared with family and friends during Hindu festivals."

"One of the ingredients is clarified butter," I said, scanning the faded handwriting, "and clarified butter is used in *diyas* like the one we found in the priest hole. It's an interesting coincidence, Emma, but——"

"It may be more than a coincidence," she interrupted. "Look at the bottom of the page."

I shifted my gaze to the bottom of the page and read aloud a single handwritten line that wasn't part of the recipe: *"April 1865. Given to me by Miss Cecilia."*

"Miss Cecilia," Emma said urgently, pointing from the recipe to the gold heart. "Could Cecilia be the *C* in 'C.M.'?"

Eleven

Emma closed the cookbook and returned it to the bookcase, but she left the recipe on the kitchen table. Tilly continued to look from the faded writing to the gleaming heart and back again. I dumped her cold tea in the sink and made a fresh pot. I could almost hear three brains whirring as I placed the teapot on the table and resumed my seat beside Emma.

"Well?" she snapped.

I'd seldom heard my friend speak so sharply. Normally, I was the impatient one, the one who jumped to conclusions with the carefree abandon of a circus acrobat, while she was the calm one, the one who thought things through before she expressed an opinion. Yet there she was, biting my head off because I hadn't jumped to a conclusion based on the flimsiest wisps of evidence. It was a striking role reversal, and I couldn't deny that it amused me greatly.

"I suppose the *C* in 'C.M.' could stand for 'Cecilia,'" I allowed.

"It must," Emma insisted. "Think about it, Lori. A Hindu altar? A superb example of Indian goldsmithing with a *C* on it? Miss Cecilia's Indian recipe? They must be connected."

"They are," said Tilly. "The thing that connects them is Anscombe Manor. Did you find any other Indian artifacts in the manor when you and Derek purchased it?"

"No," Emma replied. "The manor was virtually derelict when we moved into it. Apart from the family archives and a few forgotten odds and ends like the cookbook, it was empty. The previous owner sold the contents to cover death duties after her husband died. They were scattered to the four winds."

"A pity," said Tilly. "A portrait of Miss Cecilia Anscombe wrapped in an Indian shawl would have connected a few dots for us."

"Miss Cecilia might not have been an Anscombe," I protested. "The initials on the heart are 'C.M.,' not 'C.A.'"

"Perhaps Cecilia M. became an Anscombe through marriage," Tilly suggested.

"Let's say, for the sake of argument, that C.M. and Miss Cecilia are the same person," I said. "Why does she have to be an Anscombe?"

"Because only an Anscombe would know about the manor's priest hole," said Emma. "I can't imagine a casual visitor stumbling across it by accident. It's too well hidden."

"A casual visitor wouldn't interact with the cook, either," said Tilly.

"Excellent points," I conceded. "But the altar might not have been made by Miss Cecilia. It might have been made by a member of the Anscombe family as a tribute to Miss Cecilia."

"Well reasoned," said Tilly. "An Anscombe may have created the hidden altar as a tribute to a girl for whom he nursed a secret, perhaps a forbidden, passion."

"Aw," I said with a gusting sigh, touched by the thought of a young man nursing a secret passion. "As a lifelong romantic, I vote for Tilly's scenario. But who was Miss Cecilia? Which Anscombe fell for her? Why was their love forbidden? How did he acquire his collection of Indian artifacts? How did she acquire an Indian recipe?"

"One question at a time," Emma begged. "I'll get a headache if we tackle them all at once."

"Okay," I said. "We'll start with: Who is Miss Cecilia?"

"No idea," said Emma. "But she must have been alive in 1865, because that's when she gave the recipe to the cook."

"She had no title," Tilly observed. "She was Miss Cecilia rather than Lady Cecilia, which may indicate that her family did not belong to the aristocracy."

"Cecilia is an English name," Emma ventured. "Is it safe to assume that Miss Cecilia was English?"

"I think so," said Tilly.

"To summarize," I said. "We have an English girl from a non-aristocratic family who gave an Indian recipe to an English cook in Anscombe Manor in April 1865." When the others nodded for me to go on, I continued, "Question two: How did an English girl get hold of an Indian recipe?"

"Nothing could have been easier," Tilly said confidently. "India was under colonial rule throughout much of the nineteenth century. Benjamin Disraeli described it as the brightest jewel in the crown of the British Empire. The British maintained a considerable military, governmental, and corporate presence there, and British enclaves could be found in every corner of the subcontinent. As you can imagine, a great deal of cross-cultural pollination took place. When British soldiers, government officials, and businessmen returned to England, they often brought Indian recipes home with them."

"They must have brought other things home with them as well," said Emma.

"They did," said Tilly. "Some 'old India hands,' as they were called, filled their homes with Indian furnishings. A few built houses in the neo-Mughal style, an English interpretation of Indian architecture. Queen Victoria surrounded herself with Indian servants, and she made an effort to learn as much as she could about the culture."

I waited for a beat to make sure that she'd come to the end of her side note, then said, "Good to know, but it doesn't connect many dots for us, does it? It sounds as though Victorian England was awash in all things Indian. The recipe and the artifacts could have been acquired in England, or they could have been acquired by someone who lived in or who visited India."

"It does leave us with a rather wide range of possibilities," Tilly acknowledged apologetically.

"On to question three, then," I said after a bracing sip of tea. "What brought Miss Cecilia M. to Anscombe Manor?"

"She could have been a neighbor or a family friend," Tilly suggested. "Perhaps she went to school with an Anscombe daughter."

"Or she could have been engaged to an Anscombe son," Emma asserted. "I've never come across a Cecilia Anscombe in the family archives, but I've never had a reason to search for one." Her eyes lit up suddenly. "Kit may have heard of her, though. I'll call him."

While she spoke with Kit on her cell phone, I gave Tilly a basic outline of his complicated parentage.

"Emma's son-in-law grew up here, in Anscombe Manor," I told her. "He was raised by his late stepfather, who was an Anscombe by birth." I shrugged. "Who knows what they discussed around the dinner table?"

"I hope they discussed family history," said Tilly.

Emma ended the call and stood. "He'll be here in twenty minutes or so—enough time for us to have a quick bite of lunch. I don't know about you two, but I'm starving."

As it turned out, Tilly and I were starving, too. We slapped together a pile of sandwiches from Emma's ample supply of leftovers and polished off three of them before Kit came through the back door, smelling of horses.

"Sorry about the delay," he said. "I was up to my knees in . . . Well, let's just say that I had to change my boots and my trousers before I came indoors."

"We're grateful," I told him.

He chuckled good-naturedly as he sat next to Tilly, but he stopped laughing when he spotted the golden heart. "Early Christmas present, Emma?"

"More of a Christmas mystery," Emma replied. "Have a sandwich while I tell you about our morning."

By the time she finished describing the priest hole, the Hindu altar, the initials on the golden heart, and the addendum to the besan ladoo recipe, Kit had finished two sandwiches.

"No one mentioned the priest hole to me when I was growing up," he said ruefully. "If I'd known about it, I would have won every game of sardines I ever played in the manor."

"Did anyone mention Miss Cecilia to you?" I asked.

"Sorry," he said. "I've never heard of her, but I can confirm that an Anscombe did go to India. His name was Albert Anscombe and he was born in 1837. The only reason I know his date of birth is because it was inscribed on a portrait of him that hung in the great hall before it was shipped off to a buyer in California. Albert Anscombe cut a dashing figure, but he was a bit of a family joke."

"Why?" I asked.

Kit dusted bread crumbs from his long, slender fingers, rested his folded arms on the table, and leaned forward. "Albert was a second son. Since his older brother was destined to inherit the family estate, Albert had to choose between the only two professions that were considered acceptable in the stratified world of the minor gentry."

"The church or the army," Tilly put in, as if she was familiar with the stratified world of the minor gentry.

"After he sowed his wild oats, Albert chose the army," said Kit. "His father purchased a commission for him in the Fifty-Second (Oxfordshire) Regiment of Foot, and off he went to India."

"A famed regiment," Tilly observed, sounding impressed.

"Albert didn't contribute to their fame," Kit said with a wry smile. "He spent most of his time inspecting barracks and attending garden parties. He was decorative rather than competent, but he did his duty for an entire year before he was laid low by what was then known as a putrid fever. It could have been cholera or typhus or any one of a dozen diseases, but whatever it was, it brought him to his knees."

"He should have chosen the church," I said. "His health wouldn't have taken a hit if he'd stayed in England."

"It might have," said Tilly. "Typhoid epidemics were a common occurrence in England throughout the Victorian era. Let us not forget that Prince Albert died of typhoid fever in the Blue Room at Windsor Castle."

"Albert Anscombe didn't die," said Kit. "He came home, and although he was never a well man again, he prospered. When his older brother died in a riding accident, he became the sole heir to the Anscombe estate. He married, produced seven children, and dined out on stories about his military career for the rest of his life."

"I still don't understand why he was a family joke," I said. "He may not have been a war hero, but as you say, he did his duty."

"If he'd told the truth, we would have treated him with the respect he deserved," Kit explained. "Legend has it, however, that his tales became more and more outlandish as the years went by. Those who didn't know better were convinced that he'd led his regiment into every battle, including the Battle of Waterloo!"

I laughed, but Tilly looked perplexed.

"The Battle of Waterloo took place in 1815," she said.

Realizing that humor wasn't Tilly's strong suit, Kit explained kindly, "That's right, Tilly. The Battle of Waterloo took place before Albert Anscombe was born."

"I see," she said, her face brightening as comprehension dawned. "You were illustrating Albert's penchant for stretching the truth."

"I was," Kit acknowledged.

"I don't blame him for padding his CV," I said. "How could he tell his cronies that he'd served his country by ridding barracks of dust bunnies and dancing the night away? Leading soldiers into battle is much more respectable."

"And more entertaining," Kit said dryly.

"When did Albert go to India?" Emma inquired.

Kit shrugged. "He wore a Victorian-era uniform in his portrait, but if I ever knew the precise dates of his military service, I've forgotten them."

"And you're absolutely certain that his wife's name wasn't Cecilia?" Emma pressed.

"I am," said Kit. "I may not have a head for numbers, but I remember names. Albert married Miss Georgiana Weldstone of Weldstone Hall in Warwickshire. It was a good match. By all accounts, they were very happy together."

"I'm pleased for them," Emma said sourly, "but their story contributes nothing to the one we're attempting to unravel. Were there *any* Cecilias in your stepfather's family?"

"None that I've heard of," Kit replied, "but the Anscombe family tree has many branches. I would never pretend to know every twig."

"Perhaps Albert's wife ordered him to get rid of his Indian souvenirs," Tilly said thoughtfully, "but instead of throwing them away or selling them, he hid them in the priest hole."

"The altar looks more like a shrine than a stash," I said.

"A shrine to whom?" Emma demanded, presumably of the universe. "To Miss Cecilia? Was she Albert's lost love? Or was he hers?"

"Four questions at once!" I exclaimed, falling back in my chair. "Oh, my poor aching head!"

"Go ahead and joke," Emma said with a grudging smile, "but I intend to answer each and every one of them." She raised an eyebrow. "Are you in?"

"Need you ask?" I said. "I finished my Christmas shopping two weeks ago, and if I hang another ornament on our tree at home, it'll topple over. The church is decorated, there's no Nativity play to rehearse, and there won't be any more Christmas parties this year." I sat up and made a courteous half bow in her direction. "I'm at your service."

"Should you, perhaps, check with your husband first?" Tilly asked, eyeing me uncertainly. "You have three young children, don't you?"

"I do," I said, "and Bill is perfectly capable of looking after them. In fact, I'll be doing him a favor by making myself scarce. His job takes him away from home so often that he enjoys being a full-time dad during the holidays."

"What about you, Tilly?" Emma asked. "Are you in?"

"You'd allow me to help?" she said, as if she couldn't believe her ears.

"We're counting on you to help," I told her. "Frankly, I don't think we'd get very far without you."

"Of course you would," she said, blushing rosily, "but if you think I can be of assistance, I'll be happy to help in any way I can." She smiled shyly. "I must admit that I'd like to know more about Miss Cecilia. If she did create the Hindu altar, we intruded on a place that was sacred to her. I feel as if I owe it to her to tell her story—to make sure that she's not forgotten."

"My sentiments exactly," said Emma.

"Where will you start?" Kit inquired. "After you've shown me the priest hole, that is."

"I'll start with the archives, if I may," said Tilly.

"I'll work with you," said Emma.

"I'll call Lilian Bunting," I said.

"The vicar's wife?" Tilly asked.

"The vicar's wife who also happens to be a formidable scholar,"

I said. "If there's a Cecilia M. in the church records at St. George's, Lilian will find her."

"I'm glad you thought of Lilian," said Emma. "She forgave us for failing to wake her when Tilly rediscovered the chapel, but she'd never forgive us if we kept a priest hole and a Hindu altar to ourselves."

"She would not," Kit agreed.

"When and where shall we three meet again?" I asked, turning to Emma.

"Ten tomorrow morning?" she suggested. "Here?"

"Works for me," I said. "For now, however, I must bid you adieu. My husband is the best of men, but I don't want to push my luck. I promised him I'd be home in time for dinner."

After collecting my storage containers and taking one last look at the golden heart, I snatched up my jacket and my shoulder bag and let myself out through the back door. Unlike Mr. Barlow, I had no trouble lifting the latch.

Twelve

I came home to find Bill sprawled on the hearth rug in the living room, playing knock-down-the-wall with Bess. The game was a simple one—Bill built walls of wooden blocks and Bess knocked them down—but it was one of Bess's favorites, especially when her father played it with her. Stanley watched the action from the comfort—and safety—of Bill's favorite armchair.

The twins had sequestered themselves and their race-car track in the blanket fort they'd constructed in the dining room. Such defensive measures were necessary with a toddler in the cottage. Knock-down-the-wall was one thing. Knock-the-race-cars-off-the-track was another.

I'd arrived in plenty of time to make dinner, so I busied myself in the kitchen and had a meal on the table when the ravening horde descended, demanding sustenance. A green salad and a chicken-and-mushroom pie formed the main course, with home-made brownies à la mode for dessert. The hoard gave me rave reviews.

I would have told my nap-deprived husband about the priest hole and its many surprises after the children were asleep, but he was so tired that he went to bed when the boys did. Since it was still relatively early in the evening, I tidied the kitchen and re-stored some semblance of order to the living and dining rooms before I flopped on the sofa and called Lilian Bunting. She was thrilled by my news and eager to play a role in the search for Cecilia M.

"Submerging myself in the church records will make for a pleasant change from emptying wastebaskets filled with used tissues and listening to people describe the precise colors and textures of their bodily fluids," she said. "Forgive me if I sound unchristian."

"No one expects you to be a saint," I told her with a sympathetic chuckle.

"Anyone who did would be sorely disappointed," she returned. "I'll dive into the records first thing tomorrow morning, but I'll be at Emma's by ten, whether I find a relevant entry or not. Teddy and the Hobsons can attend to our sick parishioners without me for a few hours. A priest hole with a Hindu altar! In our parish! It's a once-in-a-lifetime discovery!"

We chatted for a few more minutes, then said good night. Though I was beginning to feel the effects of a short night and an exciting day, I pried myself from the sofa and headed for the study. I wouldn't have slept a wink if I'd gone to bed without telling Aunt Dimity about our once-in-a-lifetime discovery.

The study was still and silent. The tinsel garland I'd strung around the diamond-paned windows above the old oak desk twinkled in the light from the mantel lamps when I knelt to light a fire in the hearth. The flames seemed to dance in Reginald's black button eyes as I straightened.

"I met a wonderfully colorful elephant today," I told him. "He's a soft toy, but he's not the kind of soft toy a child would take to bed. Tilly Trout thinks he represents Ganesha, the elephant-headed son of Parvati, the Hindu goddess of love and a few other things. I don't know if there's a rabbit-headed god in the Hindu pantheon, but Tilly might. She seems to know everything about everything." I read a question in my bunny's eyes as I reached for the blue journal. "No, Reg, she doesn't know about Aunt Dimity. Some secrets are best kept to ourselves."

I touched a fingertip to his pink flannel snout, then carried the blue journal with me to one of the tall leather armchairs facing the hearth. I kicked off my shoes, braced my stockinged feet against the ottoman, rested the blue journal on my bent legs, and opened it.

"Dimity?" I said. "It's been another memorable day!"

The curving lines of royal-blue ink began to loop and curl across the blank page as soon as I finished speaking.

Good evening, Lori. Why was the day memorable? Did another car slide into one of Emma's drainage ditches?

"No," I replied. "Derek spread straw on the lane to keep everyone from crashing on the way home, and by the time I went back to Anscombe Manor, the ice had melted."

Did Bree announce her decision to return to New Zealand to nurse her broken heart?

"Bree's not going anywhere," I said flatly. "The last I heard, she was in Mr. Barlow's workshop, removing the tires from Tilly Trout's damaged car."

Has Bess learned to use the toilet?

"I'll send up fireworks when Bess's diaper days are over," I said, "and I haven't sent any up yet."

What, then, made the day memorable?

"Quite a few things," I said, "but I'll start with what will soon be the most talked-about story in Finch."

If it interests the villagers, you can rest assured that it will interest me.

"It'll knock your socks off," I assured her. I nestled the journal more comfortably on my knees and continued, "Nell's convinced that Mr. Barlow has fallen in love with Tilly Trout."

He must have fallen very quickly.

"Such things happen," I said. "Tilly has a helpless air about her, and Mr. Barlow likes to help helpless people."

True. A damsel in distress would appeal to his chivalrous nature.

"If he could have, he would have wrapped Tilly in cotton wool after the accident," I said, smiling.

Any man worth his salt would have felt protective toward Tilly.

"Would any man go out of his way to spend time with her, once she was safe and sound?" I asked. "Mr. Barlow drove to Anscombe Manor this morning to talk to her about her car, even though he could have relayed the information through Emma over the telephone."

Suggestive, but hardly conclusive.

"There's more," I said. "Before he left the manor, he offered to give Tilly a guided tour of St. George's. And as he was leaving, he fumbled with the latch on Emma's kitchen door."

He fumbled with the latch? He's clearly a man in love. I bow down to Nell's infallible intuition.

"Who doesn't?" I said dryly. "I won't be surprised if it takes Mr. Barlow a month to fix Tilly's car."

I hope, for his sake, that Tilly isn't a nun.

"She's not," I said. "When I asked her, she claimed to be nothing more than a lay member of the Church of England."

As is Mr. Barlow. So far, so good. Are his feelings reciprocated?

"I doubt it," I said. "Tilly has such a low opinion of herself that she may not believe she's lovable."

Mr. Barlow has his work cut out for him, it seems, but he's never been afraid of hard work. I hope with all my heart that his suit is successful.

"So do I, Dimity," I said. "Mr. Barlow has been alone for too long."

It sounds as though Tilly has, too. The handwriting paused for a moment, then continued to flow gracefully across the page. *As gratified as I am to be brought up to date on the latest developments in Finch, I must confess to feeling the merest whisper of disappointment. I was rather hoping your day was memorable because you found a priest hole in Emma's chapel.*

"We did find one!" I exclaimed. "To be accurate, Tilly found one. It's hidden by two panels in the wall behind the spot where the altar once stood. I thought Tilly would faint when she opened the outer panel."

Had I been in her shoes, I would have fainted. It's a remarkable discovery, Lori! What's it like inside?

"It's larger than I thought it would be," I said. "Whoever carved it out of the stone blocks behind the panels did a fine job, but it would still be a horrible place to hide. I pity the poor priests who had to stay in it for days on end while the priest hunters searched the manor. The cold and the dark would have driven me batty."

One can endure many hardships when one's life is at stake. Has Emma decided what to do with the chapel? Even if she doesn't wish to open it to the public, she might consider opening it to scholars. Architects as well as historians would stand in line to examine the priest hole.

"I doubt that she's thought that far ahead," I said. "She has something else on her mind at the moment." I took a deep breath. "The thing is, Dimity, the priest hole wasn't empty."

Oh, dear. You didn't find human remains in it, did you?

"We found something a whole lot stranger than human remains," I said. "We found a Hindu altar, complete with a bronze statue of Parvati." I could almost see the altar caught in my flashlight's quivering beam as I recounted the moment my wandering gaze fell upon the vibrant silk cloth, the scattered handfuls of rubies and emeralds, the dried garlands, the statue, the incense burner, the oil lamp, and the extraordinary elephant.

"Tilly thinks the elephant represents Ganesha," I said. I was about to explain who Ganesha was, but Aunt Dimity beat me to the punch.

It would make sense for Parvati to be accompanied by her son.

"I didn't realize that you were an expert on Hindu gods and goddesses." I said, taken aback.

I'm not an expert, Lori, but when I lived in London, I had many Indian friends, some of whom were kind enough to answer my questions about their religious beliefs.

"You've always had a hungry mind, Dimity," I observed.

An attribute we share.

"My hungry mind is stuffed to the gills at the moment," I said. "I haven't even told you about the most stunning artifact we found in the priest hole. Every object on the altar is beautiful, but the pièce de résistance has to be the golden heart that was lying beneath the elephant's trunk."

Is it like the one Bill gave you?

I put a hand to the heart-shaped locket that hung from a chain around my neck, and replied, "The gold heart we found on the altar is about a hundred times bigger than my locket, Dimity. It's not a box, and if it's a paperweight, it's the world's most expensive paperweight."

Perhaps it's an objet d'art—a beautiful object that serves no practical purpose.

"Yes," I said, nodding, "it's a sculpture in precious metal. It's made of solid gold covered in the most exquisitely intricate gold filigree, and it's easily as big as my fist. Can you imagine?"

I believe I can, thanks to your vivid description.

"There's more," I said. "Tilly believes the heart was made in India, but when we took it to the kitchen to examine it more closely, she noticed two Roman letters woven into the filigree: a *C* and an *M*. The letters reminded Emma of a recipe she found in an old handwritten cookbook a cook left behind at the manor. It's a recipe for an Indian sweet called besan ladoo, and a note at the bottom of the page explains that it was given to the cook in April 1865 by a Miss Cecilia. Emma thinks that the *C* and the *M* on the heart are Miss Cecilia's initials."

Does Emma also believe that Miss Cecilia M. concealed the Hindu altar in the priest hole?

"It's one possibility," I said. "The other is that the altar was created by Albert Anscombe, a Victorian soldier who was stationed in India, and who may have, to use Tilly's words, nursed a secret—perhaps a forbidden—passion for Cecilia."

The theory being that, upon his return from India, Albert Anscombe made the secret altar to commemorate—or possibly to celebrate—his secret love for Cecilia. Since he couldn't declare his love for Cecilia openly, I would assume that he married someone else.

"You would assume correctly," I confirmed. "Albert Anscombe married Miss Georgiana Weldstone of Weldstone Hall in Warwickshire."

When I was a child, I heard stories about a sickly major at the manor. I seem to recall Ruth and Louise Pym reminiscing about a handsome young officer whose health was ruined in a foreign land.

"They must have been speaking of Albert," I said. "He became so ill in India that he had to leave the army."

As I recall, the frail major was something of a braggart.

"Sounds like Albert," I said. "According to Kit, Albert Anscombe had a bad habit of embellishing the truth about his military service. I don't suppose the Pyms mentioned Cecilia while they were reminiscing."

I'm afraid they didn't. The handwriting paused again, then continued at a slower pace, as if Aunt Dimity was turning a notion over in her mind. *Did you say that the golden heart was positioned beneath the elephant's trunk?*

"It was behind the trunk and in front of the forelegs," I said. "Why? Does its position mean something to you?"

Perhaps. Ganesha is known as the remover of obstacles. The heart could have been offered to Ganesha by someone asking him to remove an obstacle.

"I can think of a hundred obstacles to true love," I said.

So can I, but parental disapproval was a common one in Victorian times. Albert's parents may have objected to his alliance with Cecilia, or vice versa.

"Either way, the offering to Ganesha didn't work," I said. "If the remover of obstacles had removed the obstacle, Albert would have married Cecilia. But we're getting ahead of ourselves, aren't we, Dimity? We still don't know who made the altar, or why."

Surely you intend to find out.

"Emma won't rest until we do," I said. "I don't know what's come over her, Dimity. She practically snarled at me when I pointed out a few flaws in her logic."

You were more logical than Emma?

"Believe it or not, I was," I said. "What's more, she was jumping to conclusions all over the place. I felt as if I were arguing with myself."

She's been under a great deal of pressure lately. She prepared the Christmas dinner and presided over the party, but instead of retiring to her comfortable bed at the end of the evening, she was compelled by the ice storm to play hostess to a houseful of overnight guests, one of whom will be staying with her for an indefinite period of time. She may simply be overtired.

"I get crabby when I'm overtired," I said. "Emma doesn't."

The altar is in Emma's home, Lori. She may feel personally responsible for solving the mysteries surrounding it.

"Yet another source of pressure," I said, nodding. "I guess I'll have to be the rational friend this time." I sighed. "It's a tall order."

I have faith in you, my dear. Has Emma devised a plan of attack?

"She and Tilly will trawl through the Anscombe family archives to see if they can come up with a lead on Cecilia," I said. "Lilian Bunting will do the same thing with the church records at St. George's, and we'll meet up tomorrow morning to compare notes."

What will you do?

"I'll be the rational friend," I said.

Of course you will. Honestly, Lori, I would have been satisfied with the discovery of the priest hole. To add a hidden Hindu altar and a forbidden love affair is going above and beyond the call of duty. I look forward to hearing the results of your investigation.

"It's Emma's investigation," I said, "but I'll do what I can to support her."

In the meantime, you'd better get some rest. Emma will need you to be clearheaded tomorrow. Good night, my dear.

"Good night, Dimity." I waited until the graceful handwriting faded from the page, closed the journal, and eyed Reginald doubtfully. "Me? Rational? I guess we'll just have to hope for a Christmas miracle!"

Thirteen

The fog was back on Monday morning, but my indefatigable children rose with the invisible sun. Having hit the sack early, Bill bounced out of bed, singing Christmas carols. Having chatted with Aunt Dimity until midnight, I was a bit less perky.

Bess's gummy grin revived me, as did the faint but alluring fragrance of maple syrup. By the time she and I joined Bill and the boys in the kitchen, a pancake breakfast was under way. While Bill filled our plates, I filled him in on everything that had happened at Anscombe Manor the previous day. Since Will and Rob had excellent hearing, I left out the parts about hunting, torturing, and killing human beings and described the priest hole as a place where priests could pray privately. I also made it clear to them that the chapel was strictly off limits for the time being.

"I'm sure Emma will show you the priest hole one day," I said, "but until she does, you're not to set foot in the chapel. Understood?"

"Sounds dead boring to me," said Rob. "I'd rather be riding than sitting in a cold old hole."

"I'd rather be at the stables than anywhere else in the world," Will added blithely.

"So would I," Rob agreed.

"Okay, then," said Bill. "How's this for a plan? Your mother will take you to the stables, and I'll take your sister for a ride on the steam train in Winchcombe."

"The steam train!" the twins chorused, looking chagrined.

"We didn't know about the train," said Will, sounding as if he regretted his comment about the stables.

"Santa will be there," Rob said mournfully, "with presents."

"And the train will be all lit up," Will said, toying listlessly with his pancakes.

Bill allowed them to grieve while he buttered the stack of pancakes on his plate, then said diffidently, "I don't suppose you'd like to ride the train with Bess and me, would you?"

"We would!" the boys answered instantly.

"We can go to the stables tomorrow," said Rob.

"Kit won't mind looking after Thunder and Storm for just one day," said Will.

"It's settled," said Bill, pouring a staggering amount of syrup on his pancakes. "We'll take a train ride and your mother will go to Anscombe Manor."

I felt a bit downcast myself. Had Bill informed me of his plans, I would have given Emma a rain check. A ride on the steam train was not a thing to miss at Christmastime.

"I have four tickets," Bill said tantalizingly, "and the train doesn't leave until half past noon."

"I'll be home by twelve," I said. I reached across the table and squeezed his sticky hand. "You truly are the best of husbands."

"I'm not half bad," he conceded.

THOUGH THE ICE HAD MELTED, the fog was thicker than ever. I left the cottage early because I knew it would take longer than usual to drive to Anscombe Manor. I could just barely make out the tall hedgerows that lined the narrow, twisting lane, and I didn't see Mr. Barlow's car until I reached the end of the curving drive. He'd parked it on the graveled apron, but Lilian Bunting's black BMW wasn't parked beside it. Unless she'd given Emma a fog check or hitched a ride with Mr. Barlow, I'd beaten her to the manor.

I crossed paths with Tilly Trout's suitor in the cobbled courtyard.

"Morning, Lori," he said. "I was just leaving. Nice day, isn't it?"

"Uh, sure," I said doubtfully as fingers of fog caressed my face. "How's Bree doing?"

"She banged her knuckles when she was loosening a bolt on Miss Trout's car," he said. "I had to tell her off for cursing, but she behaved herself after that."

"What I meant was—" I began, but he cut me short.

"I know what you meant," he said, "and she's doing fine in that department, too. Got a good head on her shoulders, does Bree. It'll take more than a broken engagement to break her."

"Has she talked about Jack?" I asked.

Mr. Barlow's eyebrows rose. "Why would she talk about him? Nice lad, but he wasn't the right lad for her. She needs a chap who'll stick around, not one who's flying off to God knows where every five minutes."

"Distance doesn't always make the heart grow fonder," I observed.

Mr. Barlow cleared his throat and looked away, then said with exaggerated nonchalance, "Don't think I've told you, Lori, but my sister's boy is spending Christmas with me this year."

"Is he?" I said as my gossip's antennae began to quiver.

"Driving in from Birmingham later today," said Mr. Barlow. "Shouldn't call him a boy, I suppose. He'll turn thirty in April."

"They grow up so fast," I said, recalling that Bree would turn twenty-three in March. "Will he bring his wife?"

"Doesn't have one," said Mr. Barlow. "He's good with cars, though. I've a mind to ask him to work on Miss Trout's."

"It's a big job," I said, wondering if Mr. Barlow's nephew was the kind of chap who stuck around. "An extra pair of hands would be useful."

"Can't ever have too much help," he said, nodding.

"What's your nephew's name?" I asked.

"Prescott," Mr. Barlow replied. "Thomas Prescott, but we call him Tommy."

"I look forward to meeting Tommy," I said.

"Stop by the workshop," he suggested. "I'll introduce you."

"I will," I promised, turning the names "Bree Prescott" and "Bree Pym Prescott" over in my mind.

"Better get back," said Mr. Barlow. "Good to see you, Lori."

"And you, Mr. Barlow," I said.

He strode away, whistling a jaunty tune, and I turned toward the kitchen. Before I lifted the latch, however, I gave myself a stern lecture about conclusion jumping. I couldn't claim to be Emma's rational friend if I was marrying Bree off to a guy she'd never met, so I reeled in my imagination and refrained from squealing when Mr. Barlow was safely out of earshot. Banishing all thoughts of engagement rings, wedding dresses, and christening gowns from my mind, I lifted the latch and let myself into the kitchen.

I was immediately confronted by what appeared to be a second role reversal. Emma sat at the kitchen table with her head in her hands, and Tilly sat beside her, murmuring words of encouragement. A pair of faded gray archival boxes lay before them, unopened and looking the worse for wear.

"Good morning," I said.

Emma groaned, and Tilly gave me a significant look. I had no idea what it signified, but I suspected it had something to do with the sad state of the archival boxes. I hung my jacket and shoulder bag on a hook near the door, took a clean mug from the dishwasher, slid into a chair opposite Emma, and poured myself a cup of tea from the portly brown pot on the table.

"I know I'm early," I said, "but I wanted to give myself plenty of time to get here."

"The fog is dangerously dense," Tilly remarked.

"It's a pea-souper," I agreed. Sensing her reluctance to discuss the elephant in the room, I continued, "I ran into Mr. Barlow in the courtyard."

"He came by to inform me that he was able to order the parts for my car from an automobile supply shop in Upper Deeping," said Tilly. "He intends to pick them up as soon as the fog lifts."

"Better safe than sorry," I said.

"Indeed," said Tilly. "I'd never forgive myself if my accident was the indirect cause of another."

Since Emma seemed incapable of speech, I decided to go to bat for Mr. Barlow.

"Mr. Barlow is the most sensible man I know," I said. "He wouldn't put his life on the line unless he had to, to save someone else's."

"He didn't hesitate to come to my aid," she acknowledged.

"He's always helping someone," I told her. "He looks after the whole village. When he's not replacing broken windows or oiling creaking hinges, he's mowing the lawn in the churchyard or checking the church roof for leaks. I think of him as Finch's guardian angel."

"He offered to show your church to me," said Tilly.

"I'll bet he didn't tell you that he's our sexton," I said.

"No," said Tilly, "he didn't."

"He's an usher as well," I said, hoping I wasn't laying it on too thick. "What he doesn't know about St. George's would fit in a thimble. If I were you, I'd take him up on his offer."

"I have," Tilly admitted, blushing prettily. "He'll come to fetch me at noon."

"Be sure to ask him to point out the wall paintings in St. George's," I advised. "They're world famous. Emma's husband discovered them hidden beneath a layer of plaster applied by a misguided Vic—"

"Victorian," Emma broke in despondently.

"A misguided Victorian vicar," I said, finishing my sentence. I looked uncertainly from Emma to Tilly. "Have I touched a nerve?"

"I'm afraid so," Tilly said gravely.

"It's a disaster, Lori," said Emma, raising her head from her hands. "A complete disaster."

"I'll need a few more details," I said, "because I don't know what you're talking about."

"I'm talking about water damage," she said.

She opened one of the archival boxes and pushed it across the table. I peered into it and saw a thick, misshapen wad of ink-stained pulp.

"Oh, no," I murmured.

"Oh, yes," Emma retorted miserably. "It must have happened before we replaced the roof. Derek found some water damage in the library, but I had no idea that it had wiped out the entire Victorian period."

A joke about Queen Victoria's fondness for sea bathing flitted through my mind, but I suppressed it.

"Emma's taken it very hard," said Tilly.

"She has strong feelings about paperwork," I explained.

"It's not just any old paperwork," Emma protested. "It's the section of the Anscombe family archives that would have told us about Albert Anscombe. Without it, we may never know if Albert was engaged to Cecilia before he married Georgiana."

It sounded so much like the plot of a soap opera that I had to exercise superhuman restraint to keep myself from giggling.

"I'm so sorry," I said. "Are the rest of the family records intact?"

"Yes, but they won't tell us who Cecilia is," said Emma, "or what she was doing here, in my kitchen, swapping recipes with a cook."

I didn't know what to say to her, but I told myself that Aunt Dimity was right—my friend did have a personal investment in our search for Cecilia.

"I'll make a fresh pot of tea, shall I?" said Tilly, getting to her feet.

"The sovereign remedy for all ills," I said, quoting Aunt Dimity.

"Not *this* ill," said Emma. She rested her chin in her hand and eyed the wad of paper glumly. "You've worked with old books and documents, Lori. Is there any way to recover the information written on the paper?"

"None that I know of," I said. "Not when the paper is that far gone."

Emma lapsed into an aggrieved silence I didn't dare break. The sound of the electric kettle coming to a boil seemed to reverberate through the kitchen. While Tilly filled the teapot, I racked my brain to come up with a plan B. I considered asking Ganesha to remove the water-damaged obstacle in our path, but as I wasn't Hindu, I didn't think he would listen.

It was then, when all hope seemed lost, that my cell phone rang.

Fourteen

With a muttered apology, I scrambled to my feet and ran to pull my ringing cell phone from my shoulder bag. My heart gave a hopeful leap when I saw that the caller was Lilian Bunting. Distracted by the sight of my even-tempered friend behaving like a distraught teenager, I'd completely forgotten that Lilian was our plan B.

"Lori?" she said when I answered the phone. "I'm afraid I'll have to postpone my visit to Anscombe Manor."

"Are you and the vicar okay?" I asked.

"We're fine," she said, "but my car has broken down and Mr. Barlow isn't on hand to fix it. According to Bree, he's gone to Upper Deeping for a haircut."

"Has he?" I said, with a sidelong glance at Tilly. Evidently, the fog that had prevented Mr. Barlow from retrieving the parts for her car hadn't hindered him from sprucing himself up for her. I wondered if she realized that the church tour would be their first date.

"It's this wretched virus," Lilian was saying. "If Selena Buxton wasn't unwell, she would have cut Mr. Barlow's hair, as usual. He wouldn't have had to drive all the way to the barber's in Upper Deeping." A fretful sigh escaped her. "I commend him for wanting to look his best at the Christmas service, but I do wish he'd chosen a different day to leave the village. I so wanted to see the priest hole."

"It's not going anywhere," I said.

"Nor am I," said Lilian, sounding vexed. "I'd beg a lift from Teddy, but he's visiting farms this morning, and I promised to help him with his Christmas sermon this afternoon. Would it be asking too much if I asked you, Emma, and Tilly to come to the vicarage? I'm anxious to show you an item I found in the church records last night. It concerns Cecilia."

"We'll be right over," I told her.

"Do drive carefully in front of Bree's house," Lilian pleaded. "The curve will be treacherous in the fog."

"I slid off the curve *once*," I protested. "I won't slide off it again!"

"Take it slowly," Lilian advised. "And Lori? Would you ask Emma to bring the golden heart? As I can't see the priest hole——"

"Say no more," I cut in. "We'll bring the heart." I ended the call and faced my companions, announcing exultantly, "Lilian has found Cecilia!"

EMMA PLACED A HASTY CALL to Mr. Barlow to inform him that Tilly would be at the vicarage rather than the manor. When Mr. Barlow failed to answer his phone, she left a message on his voice mail and hoped for the best.

Since I had to be home by noon or risk missing out on the steam train, we decided to take two cars. I led the way in Bill's Mercedes and Emma followed in her Land Rover, with Tilly riding shotgun.

I didn't envy Tilly. Emma, who'd been known to ride her chestnut mare through blizzards and tropical downpours, began to grumble about the fog as soon as we stepped outside. I suspected that she wouldn't stop grumbling until we reached the vicarage.

Our journey to Finch would have tried the patience of a saint, and Emma wasn't in a saintly frame of mind. When I had to feel my way around the treacherous curve in front of Bree Pym's red-brick house, I could almost hear Emma pounding the steering wheel in frustration. We must have passed the Hobsons' cottage and my father-in-law's wrought-iron gates, but I couldn't see them, and I had to slow to a crawl again as I crossed the hump-backed bridge.

If the day had been clear, the view from the top of the bridge would have warmed my heart. The village green would have stretched before me, an elongated oval of tussocky grass encircled by a cobbled lane. Evergreen wreaths and twinkling lights would have added a festive touch to the honey-colored stone buildings that lined the lane, and woodsmoke would have curled from every chimney. In the distance, St. George's stumpy, square bell tower would have played peekaboo through the boughs of the churchyard's towering cedars. Beneath me, the Little Deeping River would have leaped and gurgled between its willow-draped banks.

The day wasn't clear, however, so I had to imagine the heart-warming scene. I had to imagine the river's gurgle, too, because I wasn't about to invite the fog into my car by lowering a window. Gripping the steering wheel firmly while watching for unwary villagers, I bumped down the bridge and onto the cobbled lane.

I felt as if I were driving through a cloud. The heavy mist parted lazily as I cruised through it, then closed behind me like fuzzy gray drapes. Emma's headlights were nothing more than a pair of blurred pinpoints in my rearview mirror, and I caught only the faintest glimpses of Sally Cook's tearoom, Bill's office, and old Mrs. Craven's cottage as they loomed intermittently out of the fog.

Prior experience rather than eyesight told me I'd passed the old schoolhouse that would have been the venue for the Nativity play, and the schoolmaster's house where George Wetherhead lived. I released a sigh of relief when I pulled up in front of the vicarage, then braced myself for impact as Emma pulled up behind me. I heaved a second sigh of relief when she parked the Land Rover without putting a dent in Bill's bumper.

It wasn't until we were standing in the vicarage's front garden that I could make out the twinkling lights in the windows and the holly wreath on the front door. Lilian must have been watching for us, because she opened the door before we reached it. Emma brushed past me impatiently, and Tilly, who looked as though she was glad to be on terra firma again, trailed after her. I followed them inside.

Angel, the fluffy white vicarage cat, seemed to sense Emma's prickly mood, because she put her head out of the dining room, then beat a hasty retreat. Lilian, who was dressed in a tweed skirt, a pearl-gray twinset, and tasseled loafers, seemed to sense Emma's mood as well, because she didn't offer us tea or waste time chatting about the weather. After collecting our coats, she ushered us into the library at the rear of the rambling two-story house.

The book-lined room stretched the full width of the vicarage. Its mullioned windows and French doors overlooked a broad meadow that sloped down to the riverbank. The vicar's mahogany desk stood before the French doors, but it faced into the room, as though he preferred the sight of books to the sight of a water-logged meadow.

Every lamp in the library had been lit, presumably to fend off the encroaching gloom, and a log fire burned in the modest stone hearth, bathing the room in warmth. A green velvet sofa sat at a right angle to the hearth, facing a pair of comfortably saggy armchairs across an old coffee table. Tilly and I took the armchairs, and Emma sat beside Lilian on the sofa.

Lilian began to reach for a red spiral-bound notebook that lay on the coffee table, then stopped with a gasp as Emma held the golden heart out to her. Lilian took it and turned it over in her hands, allowing the flickering firelight to play on its intricate surface.

"Exquisite," she said as she returned the heart to Emma. "Valuable, as well, though I suspect its owner cared more about the giver than the gift."

"Do you know who gave the heart to whom?" Emma asked eagerly.

"Not yet, but it must have been a gift given with love," Lilian replied, "and love is always more valuable than gold."

"Yes, it is," Emma agreed, though she sounded as if she would have preferred a positive response to a platitude. With a sigh, she placed the heart on the coffee table, with the entwined *C* and *M* facing upward.

"Did you find any useful information in the Anscombe family archives?" Lilian inquired.

Emma groaned and buried her face in her hands, so I told Lilian about the water-damaged papers.

"Which is why we're kind of counting on you," I concluded, adding in a stage whisper, "If you haven't found anything, make something up. Emma needs a win."

Emma lifted her head and nodded wearily. "Lori's right, Lilian. I do need a win."

"Please don't get your hopes up *too* high," Lilian cautioned, "because there may be a slight hitch." She picked up the red notebook and opened it. "I copied the relevant entries from the church records verbatim, but to save time I'll summarize them for you." She glanced down at her notes. "Albert Anthony Anscombe was the second of five children born to Sir Stanley and Lady Margaret Anscombe. The Anscombes had two sons and three daughters. None of the daughters were named Cecilia."

"Kit told us he'd never heard of a Cecilia Anscombe," I said.

"I couldn't find one in the records," said Lilian, "and I went all the way back to the sixteen hundreds."

"How late did you stay up last night?" I asked, taken aback.

"Quite late," she replied. "There wasn't anything else to do, and once I get stuck in to a project, I find it hard to stop." She consulted her notes again. "Albert Anscombe was christened in St. George's Church on the fifteenth of July, 1837. His name doesn't surface again until the banns were read in 1865."

"The banns?" I said uncomprehendingly.

"The banns of marriage," Lilian clarified.

For the first time since we'd entered the vicarage, Tilly spoke up. "The word 'banns' is taken from a Middle English word meaning 'proclamation,' which is rooted in Frankish and thus can be traced back to Old French."

"Fascinating," I said, "but not entirely helpful."

"Honestly, Lori," Lilian said with a hint of exasperation. "Teddy has presided over several weddings since you moved to Finch, including yours. You and Bill used a special license to get married, but you must remember Teddy reading the banns before the other weddings."

The vicar was a lovely man, but there was no getting around the fact that his sermons were soporific rather than stimulating. I couldn't bring myself to tell Lilian that I allowed my mind to wander freely whenever her husband climbed into the pulpit, however, so I said with more kindness than truth, "I remember hearing the banns, but I've never really understood them."

Lilian's pursed lips and cocked head suggested that she saw through the kindness, but she didn't call me out on my lie.

"Banns are an announcement of a couple's intention to marry," she explained. "They must be read aloud in the home churches of both parties and in the church in which they are to be married, if it differs from their home churches. The banns must be read out in church on three Sundays in the three months prior to the wedding."

"For a marriage to be lawful in the Church of England," Tilly added, "banns must be read out in church."

"Why?" I asked.

"They're a safeguard against invalid marriages," said Lilian. "When the banns are read, anyone can come forward with a reason why the proposed marriage may not lawfully take place."

"Impediments to marriage vary between legal jurisdictions," Tilly chimed in, "but they normally include a preexisting marriage that has been neither dissolved nor annulled—"

"A vow of celibacy or a lack of consent," Lilian interjected.

"Or the couple being related within prohibited degrees of kinship," Tilly finished.

It was like watching a scholarly tennis match, but between the two of them, I had my explanation.

"Got it," I said. "Carry on!"

"Finally," Emma muttered.

Lilian turned a page in the notebook and continued, "On the fifth of March and on the second of April, 1865, the banns were read——"

"Miss Cecilia's recipe for besan ladoo is dated 1865," I broke in.

"For pity's sake, Lori," Emma said waspishly. "Will you please stop interrupting Lilian?"

"Sorry," I mumbled. "Go ahead, Lilian."

Lilian began again. "On the fifth of March and on the second of April, 1865, the banns were read for the marriage between Albert Anthony Anscombe of this parish and Cecilia Rose Pargetter of the parish of Skeaping."

I did not cry out, *"Cecilia!"* But I thought it.

"The banns were read twice," said Lilian, "but they weren't read a third time, and there's no record of the marriage taking place in St. George's." She looked up from her notes. "Albert Anscombe's name doesn't appear again in the church records until the banns are read for his marriage to Miss Georgiana Weldstone. Albert and Georgiana were married in St. George's on the seventeenth of June, 1866."

"What happened?" I asked. "Why didn't Albert marry Cecilia? Did he jilt her when he met Georgiana?"

"She could have jilted him," Lilian pointed out.

"Someone could have unearthed an impediment that barred them from marrying each other," Tilly offered.

"Or they could have agreed that they'd made a mistake," said Lilian, "and gone their separate ways amicably."

"Whatever happened," Emma said tiredly, "it has nothing to do with the Hindu altar in my priest hole. Albert's Cecilia was Cecilia *Pargetter*." She pointed at the entwined initials on the gold heart. "And 'Pargetter' doesn't begin with *M*."

"That's the hitch," said Lilian.

I stared at the heart, willing my brain to come up with a solution that would put Emma out of her misery. Happily, it obliged.

"Maybe it's not a hitch," I said slowly.

"What do you mean?" asked Lilian.

"We've been assuming that Miss Cecilia's initials are C.M.," I said. "What if they aren't? What if the *M* doesn't refer to Cecilia but to someone who gave the gold heart to her as a memento of their love?"

"Are you suggesting that someone other than Albert gave the gold heart to Cecilia?" said Emma. "Someone whose name begins with *M*?"

"Why not?" I said. "Put yourself in Cecilia's shoes. You're engaged to be married to Albert when you fall hopelessly in love with M. What do you do? Your parents will look at you cross-eyed if you break up with Albert, so you commemorate your love for M. with an altar in the priest hole."

"How did Cecilia find out about the priest hole?" Emma asked.

"The cook told her about it when they were swapping recipes," I said, struck by sudden inspiration. Hoping that no one would ask me how the cook knew about the priest hole, I continued. "Maybe Cecilia planned to visit the altar secretly after she was married, for old time's sake, but when the marriage fell through and she was banned from the manor, she couldn't retrieve her treasures."

"Perhaps M. was the reason the marriage fell through," Lilian said thoughtfully. "Perhaps he stood up in church during the reading of the banns and declared his undying love for Cecilia."

"After which, he galloped away with her on a white horse," I said triumphantly, "and they lived happily ever after." I looked at Emma. "Satisfied?"

"No," she replied, frowning. "It's a nice story, but it's completely hypothetical. We have to find out more about Cecilia Pargetter. We have to find out who M. is."

Her unremitting sullenness was beginning to get on my nerves, but I reminded myself of all the times she'd put up with my moods, took a deep breath, and said calmly, "Of course we do."

"Well," said Lilian, perusing her notes, "we know that Cecilia Pargetter was 'of the parish of Skeaping.'"

"Skeaping?" I said as a memory clicked into place. "I've been to Skeaping Manor. Bree and I took the boys there before Bess was born. It's a museum now, but it was a house once. Maybe Cecilia Pargetter lived in Skeaping Manor."

"Where is Skeaping Manor?" Emma asked.

"It's about three miles south of Upper Deeping," I said, "on the edge of Skeaping village."

"We could ring the museum," Tilly said tentatively. "The curator would be able to tell us about the manor's previous occupants."

"He would," I agreed, "but the museum is closed for the holidays."

"We don't need a curator," Emma said determinedly. "We need a computer."

"Feel free to use my laptop," said Lilian. "It's on Teddy's desk. While you're conducting your search, I'll make tea."

If anyone could track down Cecilia Pargetter of Skeaping parish on the internet, it was Emma, but though she tapped and muttered for a solid twenty minutes, she came up empty. By the time she returned to the sofa, she needed the consoling cup of tea Lilian poured for her.

"Don't throw in the towel just yet," Lilian told her. "I've thought of another resource we can utilize."

"What's that?" said Emma.

"The *Upper Deeping Dispatch*," Lilian replied. "It's a local newspaper, and Skeaping is a local village. The *Dispatch* prints announcements about all sorts of things, including births, deaths, and—"

"Marriages!" Emma exclaimed, spilling her tea.

"Kit and I used the archives once," I said. "We found exactly what we needed, but we weren't searching for information from the mid-nineteenth century. How long has the *Dispatch* been in operation?"

"It was established in 1821," said Lilian.

"Nearly twenty years before Albert Anscombe was born," said Emma, whose number skills were superior to Kit's.

"They haven't digitized the older editions yet," said Lilian, "but we can search the original newspapers by hand."

"Is the *Dispatch* open today?" Emma asked as she blotted the spilled tea with a napkin. "Or is it closed for the holidays?"

"The archives are always open to me," Lilian said, smiling. "The newspaper's owner and publisher is a dear friend of mine.

When she became aware of my interest in local history, she gave me a set of keys to the building. I can explore the archives whenever I like."

"I'm afraid I won't be able to explore them with you today," Tilly said reluctantly.

"I'll have to bow out, too," I said.

"So will I," said Lilian. Before Emma could accuse us of being traitors, Lilian assumed the businesslike manner that made her so effective at defusing quarrels during committee meetings. "Will everyone be free tomorrow? Good. It would be best if we traveled together in one car."

I nodded. "Parking spaces are at a premium during the Christmas rush in Upper Deeping."

"Lori will drive," Lilian stated firmly. "My car is out of commission, and you'll forgive me for saying so, Emma, but Bill's Mercedes is more comfortable than your Land Rover."

"Do you hear me arguing?" Emma asked.

"I'll pick you and Tilly up at ten," I said, "then swing into the village to fetch Lilian. We'll be in Upper Deeping"—I remembered the fog and revised my estimated time of arrival—"when we get there."

"Wear old clothes," Lilian advised. "The archives aren't dusted regularly, or ever, really."

"I'm afraid I didn't bring any old clothes with me," Tilly said apologetically.

"I'll find some for you," said Emma.

I raised my teacup and said, "A toast to better luck tomorrow!"

"To better luck tomorrow!" the others chorused, raising their cups.

We'd begun to discuss lunch when the doorbell rang. Lilian left the library to answer it, and Tilly, looking flustered, consulted her wristwatch.

"That will be Mr. Barlow," she said.

"It can't be twelve o'clock!" I cried, though the chiming mantel clock begged to differ. I grabbed my shoulder bag and jumped to my feet, but I knew it was already too late to make it to the cottage before Bill left for the train station. I would have sullied Tilly's chaste ears with rude remarks about the fog if Bill hadn't chosen that moment to call my cell phone.

"We're at Anscombe Manor," he said. "Where are you?"

"The vicarage," I replied.

"Stay put," he said. "I'm on my way."

"Honestly, Bill," I said, "you are the best—"

"I'd have to be a pretty lousy husband to forget how easily you lose track of time," Bill interrupted. "Be ready to leave when we get there, okay?"

"I will," I promised, and ended the call.

While I'd been on the phone with my husband, Tilly had gone to meet her swain. I dropped my phone into my bag, said a quick good-bye to Emma, and raced to the hall closet to fetch my jacket. When I got there, I found Lilian standing in the front doorway, watching Mr. Barlow escort Tilly through the garden.

"It seems there's more than one reason to get a haircut," she observed quietly.

"If I were the vicar," I murmured, "I'd get ready to read the banns again in St. George's."

Fifteen

We had a wonderful time on the steam train. The fog fell away as the gleaming black engine climbed out of the river valley, and the sun emerged from its cloudy cloak to kiss the rolling hills and the patchwork fields. Bill and I savored the views when we caught a glimpse of them, but we spent most of our time enjoying our children's enjoyment.

The driver allowed Will and Rob to ride with him in the engine, and glory of glories, the stoker permitted them to shovel coal into the firebox. Bess lurched like a drunken sailor as she marched up and down the aisle, peering curiously at our fellow passengers. I maintained a tight grip on her hands to keep her from tumbling under their feet until she clambered onto our empty seat and settled in for a nap. Lulled by the train's rocking motion and by the clickety-clack of the wheels rolling over the track, I came very close to following her example.

Our visit to Santa's grotto began well. The boys were far too mature to even consider sitting on his lap, but they weren't too old to accept the train-engine-shaped pencil sharpeners and the gaily wrapped chocolates Santa's helpers presented to them. Their sister's encounter with Santa was more problematic.

Bess would have nothing to do with the white-bearded one until he ignored her, at which point she strode boldly up to him and attempted to pull off his beard. It would have been funny if the beard had been fake, but unfortunately, it was not. Her victim knew better than to put up a struggle, and I disentangled her fingers before she did any lasting harm. Even so, I wouldn't have blamed Santa's helpers if they'd given my darling daughter a lump of coal. They were too kind to punish a toddler for acting her age, however, and she walked away with a little red teddy bear.

After a blissfully uneventful dinner at a restaurant in Winchcombe, we returned to the vicarage, where I'd left Bill's car. I kept an eye out for Mr. Barlow and Tilly while I transferred from one vehicle to the other, but if they were strolling hand in hand across the village green, I couldn't see them. With no ears to sully, I expressed my opinion of the fog in fulsome terms as I followed my family home.

While the boys played with the train set their grandfather had given them the previous Christmas, I took Bess upstairs for story time in the nursery. She was so tuckered out by then that a short story sufficed. After she was nestled all snug in her crib, I joined my menfolk on the living room floor.

Bill listened attentively while I told him about the progress we'd made in our search for Cecilia. When I mentioned the upcoming trip to the *Upper Deeping Dispatch*, he agreed that it was necessary, if only to keep Emma from grinding her teeth down to stubs. He was undaunted by the prospect of spending more time on his own with the children.

"We had a big day today," he said, "so tomorrow will be low-key. The stables will do. Rob and Will can exercise their ponies, and Bess and I can commune with Toby." Toby was an elderly pony whose easygoing disposition made him a great favorite among very, very young equestrians. "We'll have lunch at the tea-room, I think. Henry Cook needs the company."

I kissed him soundly, then repaired to the study for an early chat with Aunt Dimity. As Bill had said, it had been a big day. I didn't think I could stay awake until midnight.

Reginald's black button eyes reminded me of the gleaming black locomotive as I knelt to light a fire in the hearth. He seemed pleased to hear about Bess's little red bear, and amused by my description of her wrestling match with Santa. My bunny had a kind heart, but he also had a mile-wide mischievous streak.

After giving his pink flannel ears a twiddle, I sat in a tall leather armchair facing the hearth, collected my thoughts, which were many and varied, and opened the blue journal to a blank page.

"Aunt Dimity?" I said. "Cupid is alive and well in Finch."

I smiled as Aunt Dimity's elegant script began to unfurl across the page.

Good evening, Lori. I presume you're referring to Cupid's arrow striking Mr. Barlow.

"I'm referring to Mr. Barlow himself," I told her. "He's invited his grown-up nephew to spend Christmas with him. It must have been a last-minute invitation, because I didn't know about it until today."

Are you implying that he issued the invitation after he heard about Bree's broken engagement?

"I wouldn't put it past him," I said. "He's awfully fond of Bree."

One assumes he's fond of his nephew, too. What have you learned about the young man?

"His name is Tommy Prescott, he lives in Birmingham, he's single, and he likes to work on cars," I said. "Mr. Barlow didn't say it outright, but he hinted that Tommy's a Steady Eddie who'd rather stay close to home than live out of a suitcase."

How old is Tommy Prescott?

"He'll turn thirty in April," I said, adding with a sly grin, "In case you've forgotten, Bree will turn twenty-three in March."

Not too many years between them, nor too few. Moreover, they share an interest in repairing things, as well as a fondness for home and hearth. Clever old Mr. Barlow. From now on, I shall envision him with a tiny bow and a quiver of arrows.

"And wings," I said, laughing. "Don't forget the wings."

I'd never forget the wings! When will Tommy arrive in Finch?

"He should be here already," I said. "I'll try to check him out tomorrow."

I look forward to hearing your assessment.

"If Tommy takes after his uncle," I said, "Bree would be lucky to have him."

She most assuredly would. And he, of course, would be lucky to have her. I thought Mr. Barlow's company would be good for Bree, but I must confess that I didn't expect him to find a suitable young man for her before the week was out.

"I'll bet he chose Tommy for Bree a long time ago," I said, "and vice versa. He couldn't bring Tommy to Finch until Jack was out of the picture, but as soon as Jack was gone, he got on the phone to Tommy. You know what, Dimity?" I watched two flames leap high above the others in the fire. "I'm beginning to agree with you. Jack may have done Bree a favor by breaking up with her."

We shall see. I hope Mr. Barlow's foray into matchmaking hasn't distracted him from his pursuit of Tilly Trout.

"He showed her around St. George's this afternoon," I said. "I couldn't sneak into the church to spy on them because—" I broke off as Aunt Dimity's handwriting flew across the page.

Because you're not the kind of woman who sneaks around in order to spy on her friends and neighbors. Correct?

"Uh, yes," I said hastily, casting a guilty glance at Reginald. "But I also wanted to ride on the steam train with Bill and the children."

The steam train? How jolly! Did you visit Father Christmas, too?

"We did," I replied. I launched into a detailed account of our railroading adventure and our ill-fated trip to Santa's grotto, concluding with "I'll put mittens on Bess before we go there next year."

I'm sure she wasn't the first child to tug on the poor fellow's beard, but I'm equally certain that he'll be relieved to see the mittens. It sounds as though you had a splendid day, my dear.

"I haven't told you about the first half of it yet," I said. "I'm pleased to report that there have been several developments in the Cecilia saga. I no longer believe, for example, that the letters on the gold heart correspond to her initials. I think the *C* and the *M* form a monogram linking Cecilia's name to the name of the person who gave the heart to her."

An interesting theory. Do you have evidence to support it?

"Sort of," I said.

Close enough. Proceed!

I began at the beginning, with the water-damaged papers Emma had uncovered in the Anscombe family archives, then skipped ahead to focus on what I considered to be the most pertinent piece of information Lilian had retrieved from the church records: the incomplete reading of the banns of marriage between

Albert Anthony Anscombe and Cecilia Rose Pargetter of Skeaping parish.

"The banns prove that Cecilia Pargetter was engaged to Albert Anscombe in 1865," I said. "We know that the engagement gave Cecilia access to Anscombe Manor because she gave the besan ladoo recipe to the cook in 1865."

It's possible that she had access to the manor long before her engagement to Albert. If she and Albert belonged to the same social milieu, they could have known each other since childhood.

"Children are always getting into places they shouldn't," I said, recalling a certain incident that involved my sons, the church tower, and a bag full of water balloons. "Cecilia could have discovered the priest hole by accident when she was a little girl. Years later, when she was a young woman on the verge of marriage, it would have struck her as the perfect place to hide things she couldn't share with her future husband."

Such as gifts from a former beau whose first name began with M?

"Exactly," I said. "I think—and Lilian agrees with me—that M. could be the reason the marriage never took place. The sudden reappearance of an old flame would explain why the banns weren't read a third time. And if Cecilia broke up with Albert in order to marry M., she would have had to forfeit the treasures she'd placed in the priest hole."

Yes, I see. You've made the pieces fit together very nicely, my dear, but the picture won't be complete unless you prove that Cecilia Pargetter married M.

"I'm way ahead of you, Dimity," I said. "Emma, Lilian, Tilly, and I are going to Upper Deeping tomorrow to mine the *Dispatch*'s archives."

An excellent plan. Cecilia Pargetter of Skeaping parish was a local girl. The Dispatch *should contain a wealth of information about her and her family.*

"I'll be looking for a marriage announcement that reveals M.'s true identity," I said. "I can't wait to find out what the *M* stands for. Montague? Mungo? Marmaduke? I'm kind of hoping for something more colorful than Matthew or Mark."

I suggest that you examine the obituaries as well.

"Why?" I asked.

The sudden reappearance of an old flame may not explain why the banns of marriage weren't read a third time. I'm sorry to say it, but it's also possible that death intervened. Cecilia could have fallen from her horse or succumbed to any number of diseases. It's not a cheerful thought, I know, but it's one that must be considered.

"If we can't find a marriage announcement," I said with a melancholy sigh, "we'll look for Cecilia in the obituaries."

If it's not too much to trouble, I'd appreciate it if you'd satisfy my curiosity while you're reading old editions of the Dispatch.

"Curiosity about what?" I asked.

I'd like to know if Cecilia traveled to India. When England still had an empire, it wasn't unusual for girls from well-to-do families to sail to the ends of the earth—properly chaperoned, of course. Cecilia's parents might have sent her to India to be introduced to her fiancé's friends and fellow officers. If she did go abroad, her parents would almost certainly have announced her departure and her return in the local newspaper. In those days, the Dispatch *would have had a regular column listing the comings and goings of local travelers.*

"Maybe M. was a fellow officer," I said as my imagination took flight. "Maybe he and Cecilia fell madly in love while she was visiting Albert in India, but he couldn't obtain leave to return to England until the banns had already been read twice. Before the vicar could read them a third time, M. charged into St. George's in his scarlet tunic and declared his love for her, putting an end to one marriage and getting the ball rolling on another." I smiled ruefully. "I hope so, anyway. A wedding would be cheerier than a funeral."

You've always had a soft spot for happy endings. To ensure that you, Emma, Lilian, and Tilly have one tomorrow, I'd advise you to consult the weather forecast before you leave in the morning. None of you will be happy if you're marooned in Upper Deeping by another ice storm!

I laughed as the handwriting faded from the page, but as soon as I returned the blue journal to its place on the bookshelves, I used Bill's laptop to scan the forecasts for ice storms.

Sixteen

Bill and I woke the following morning to the miraculous sight of sunlight falling through our bedroom windows. It wasn't falling very hard, but a weak, watery sun was better than no sun at all. Sometime in the night, the fog had lifted, leaving behind a damp but visible world. When Bill bounced out of bed singing "Deck the Halls," I sang with him.

To get his low-key day off to a low-key start, I made oatmeal for breakfast, but I sprinkled it with raisins, chopped figs, and chopped walnuts to keep it interesting.

Between spoonfuls, the boys spoke of nothing but Thunder and Storm, and Bess responded to every question with "Toby!" Bill took the hint and left for Anscombe Manor before I did. I finished my oatmeal and tidied the kitchen at a leisurely pace I enjoyed but seldom experienced.

Mindful of Lilian's warning, I dressed in an old flannel shirt and an ancient pair of blue jeans before I hopped into the Mercedes and headed for the manor. The brief journey was less life-threatening than it had been the day before, thanks to the fog's departure. As I turned into the manor's curving drive, I gave a grateful thumbs-up to the sun.

Emma must have been watching for my arrival, because she and Tilly were halfway down the broad stone staircase before I switched off the engine. They, too, had chosen to wear blue jeans for our dusty day in the archives, but the rolled cuffs on Tilly's indicated that she'd borrowed hers from Emma. Emma wasn't a towering Amazon by any means, but even she was taller than Tilly. Emma had thrown on an old barn jacket, but Tilly had chosen to wear her own black coat. A wintry sunbeam picked out the mourning brooch pinned to the collar.

When Tilly insisted on riding in the backseat, Emma didn't argue. The look on her face told me that she'd abandoned her stalwart attempts to bolster Tilly's sense of self-worth.

"What do you think of our church?" I asked Tilly.

"It's wonderful," she replied, "and Mr. Barlow's knowledge of it is quite profound. He pointed out architectural features I wouldn't have noticed, and he knew the stories behind every monument in the churchyard."

Clever old Mr. Barlow, I thought, giving him a mental pat on the back. Aloud I said, "What did you do after you left St. George's?"

"We had tea and crumpets at the tearoom," she said. I could almost feel her blush as she added, "He insisted on paying our bill. He's a true gentleman, and I had a most pleasant afternoon in his company."

"I'm glad you enjoyed it," I said, grinning from ear to ear.

The sunnier weather allowed Emma and me to point out local landmarks to our guest as we drove to the village, and I paused at the top of the humpbacked bridge to allow her to take in the view.

While Tilly feasted her eyes on Finch, my gaze was drawn inexorably to the unfamiliar car parked in front of Mr. Barlow's workshop. I was so absorbed in debating whether or not the unassuming sedan might belong to Tommy Prescott that Emma had to remind me to drive on.

When we reached the vicarage, Emma and Tilly elected to stay in the car while I ran through the front garden and knocked on the door. The vicar opened it, looking vaguely worried.

"I'm afraid my wife may be a few minutes late," he said. "She's on the telephone with Opal Taylor. Apparently, there's been some confusion regarding a bill Lilian may have forgotten to post."

Since Opal Taylor was a champion talker, I decided to make the most of Lilian's misfortune.

"Not to worry," I assured him. "Tell Lilian to take her time. We're in no hurry." My words did not suit my actions, however, as I spun on my heel and dashed back to the car to explain the situation to Emma.

"Opal Taylor?" she said with a groan. "She'll talk Lilian's ear off. We won't get away until noon."

"I'm sure Lilian will try to cut the call short," I said. "In the meantime, sit tight. I'll be right back."

Before Emma could ask where I was going—or order me to stay—I loped across the squelchy green to knock on the door of Mr. Barlow's workshop. Happily, he answered it within seconds.

"Been running, Lori?" he asked as I tried to catch my breath. "The Mercedes hasn't broken down, has it? Miss Trout told me you were taking her and Emma and Mrs. Bunting to Upper Deeping this morning."

"I am," I said. "The car's fine, but Lilian's on the phone with Opal Taylor—"

Mr. Barlow rolled his eyes.

"—so I thought I'd put the delay to good use." I gestured toward the unfamiliar, small sedan. "Tommy's?"

"Yep," said Mr. Barlow. "Got in last night. Hold on a tick. I'll give him a shout. He's gapping the plugs from Mrs. Bunting's car." Mr. Barlow turned his head and bellowed into the workshop, "Tommy? Come here, lad! There's someone I'd like you to meet."

A moment later Mr. Barlow stepped outside to make room for his nephew, who seemed to fill the doorway. Tommy Prescott was a strapping lad. He was so tall that he had to duck to avoid banging his head on the lintel, and I doubted that there was an ounce of fat on his majestic body.

There were scars on it, though—a long, ragged one on his left cheek, and a smaller, neater one above his left eye. His dark hair was shaved so close to his scalp that I could make out a third scar that ran from his left temple to a spot just above his left ear. I wondered if he'd gone through the windshield in a car accident and thought again of how fortunate Tilly had been to escape her crash unscathed.

Tommy's chiseled features would have been severe if they hadn't been softened by a pair of kindly brown eyes and a mouth that curved easily into a slow, sweet smile. The state of his clothes suggested that his uncle had put him to work bright and early. His sweatshirt and blue jeans were stained with axle grease, and his sneakers bore traces of motor oil.

"Tommy," said Mr. Barlow, "this is Lori Shepherd."

"I'm pleased to meet you," said Tommy. His deep voice washed over me like melted chocolate. "I'd shake your hand, but I don't think you'll want to shake mine." He displayed his grease-streaked palms.

"Maybe next time," I said, smiling. "And please, call me Lori."

"I will," he said amiably. "Uncle Bill has told me a lot about you, including the fact that you go by your first name so you won't have to explain why you didn't take your husband's last name."

His detailed knowledge of my personal life came as no surprise to me. The village grapevine had a long reach.

"He hasn't told me very much about you," I said. "How long do you plan to stay in Finch?"

"Through New Year's," Tommy replied. "Longer, if Uncle Bill will have me."

"Don't be stupid, lad," said Mr. Barlow. "You know you're welcome to stay as long as you like."

Bree's voice blared suddenly from within the workshop. "Tom! Where did you put the crosshead screwdriver?"

"In my pocket!" Tommy hollered back. He pulled the screwdriver from his back pocket and grinned. "I'd best bring the crosshead to the boss before she loses her temper. She has a short fuse, that one. Keeps me on my toes. Great to meet you, Lori."

"And you, Tommy," I said.

As he stepped back through the doorway, I noticed that he walked with a slightly uneven gait. Mr. Barlow must have followed my gaze, because he answered the question I was too polite to ask.

"Tommy joined the army when he was eighteen," he said as soon as his nephew was out of earshot. "Served in Afghanistan. One of those roadside bombs you hear about on the news exploded not ten yards away from him. Lost his left leg below the knee. Banged his head up pretty good, too."

"I'm so sorry," I said.

"Don't be," said Mr. Barlow. "Could've been worse. Could've died. The explosion killed four of his mates."

Words failed me. I reached out to grasp Mr. Barlow's hand, then jumped as someone—meaning Emma—leaned on the Mercedes's horn.

"I've got to go," I said reluctantly. "Does everyone else in Finch know what happened to Tommy?"

"No," said Mr. Barlow. "The lad asked me to keep it to myself, so I did."

"Am I allowed to talk about it?" I asked.

"Tell whoever you like," he said. "I wouldn't have told you if I didn't expect every living soul in the village to hear about it before nightfall. I'm hoping to spare Tommy the trouble of answering a load of damn-fool questions."

The horn sounded again. I gave Mr. Barlow's hand a quick squeeze and jogged back to the Mercedes, wondering if Lilian, Tilly, or the vicar would mind if I left Emma at the vicarage.

I DIDN'T TELL the others about Tommy Prescott straightaway. I had to wait for Emma to stop scolding me for wasting time, and for Lilian to stop scolding herself for taking Opal Taylor's call.

"I should have known better than to pick up the phone when I had an appointment to keep," Lilian said from the backseat. "I could have kicked myself when I heard Opal's voice."

"A common reaction," I said, but my quip went unnoticed.

"Sick people can be fretful, " Lilian allowed, "and she's still very weak, but to accuse me of forgetting to post her water bill is the outside of enough. I've never forgotten to post a bill in my life."

Emma and I made a concerted effort to soothe her injured pride, and eventually she stopped seething.

"Subject closed," she said sheepishly. "My apologies for foisting my indignation on you. Let's move on to a more pleasant topic, shall we? Who, for example, is the handsome young man you were chatting with, Lori? I don't recall seeing him before."

"He's Mr. Barlow's nephew," I said. "His name is Tommy Pres—"

"Not little Tommy?" Lilian interrupted incredulously.

"He's not little anymore," said Emma.

"No, indeed," said Lilian, "but I've known Tommy since he was a boy. He used to visit his uncle every summer. The last time I saw him, he was a gangly teenager."

"He's filled out," said Emma. "If he wants to ride, I'll have to borrow a horse from another stable, because none of mine are big enough for him."

"I don't think he'll want to ride," I said. "He's been through a lot since he was a gangly teenager. . . ." When I finished telling them about Tommy Prescott's military service and his injuries, I heard Lilian release a mournful sigh.

"I understand now why it took him so long to return to Finch," she said. "First an overseas posting, then a brain injury and a shattered leg . . . Rehabilitation can take years if it's done properly, and all too often it's not. We'll have to do our best to make him feel welcome in our village."

"How do we keep our less tactful neighbors from staring at his artificial leg?" Emma asked.

"They won't stop staring at his prosthetic until it loses its novelty value," Lilian replied wisely. "I hope he stays with his uncle long enough for everyone to grow accustomed to it."

"If Mr. Barlow has his way," I said, "Tommy will stay in Finch for the rest of his life."

"What do you mean?" Lilian asked.

"Bree," I said.

"Oh," said Lilian, drawing the simple syllable out to twice its normal length. "So that's the plan, is it? It's a very good one."

"Let's hope Bree agrees," said Emma.

"Only time will tell," I said, "but if I were Bree, I'd—" I broke off before I could scandalize Tilly. "I'd be happy to make a new friend."

"Uh-huh," said Emma sarcastically, giving me a sidelong look.

"Forgive me for asking," said Tilly, "but is Bree the dark-haired young woman who assists Mr. Barlow?"

"That's Bree," I said.

Lilian, Emma, and I whiled away the rest of the trip by filling Tilly in on Bree's troubled past, the tragedy that brought her from New Zealand to Finch, and her recently broken engagement, thus proving that gossip, like Cupid, was alive and well in Finch.

Seventeen

Upper Deeping exuded Christmas cheer. Evergreen garlands topped with shiny red bows adorned the lamp posts, strings of twinkling snowflakes hung high above the streets, and holiday displays filled the shop windows. A beautifully decorated tree stood in the main square, where a choir dressed in Victorian garb serenaded passersby and an open-air Christmas market tempted them with food, drink, and a glittering array of festive trinkets.

Emma grumbled about the heavy traffic and the shoals of harried shoppers, but I thought they added just the right touch of madness to the week before Christmas. After driving in stop-and-go circles for twenty minutes, I pulled into a parking space three blocks away from our destination.

The offices of the *Upper Deeping Dispatch* were located in a building just off the main square. Had I been on my own, I would have treated myself to a bag of roasted chestnuts from the open-air market, but I didn't wish to be accused of wasting more time, so I postponed my treat.

Lilian's set of keys enabled us to enter the building through a back door. From there, she led us down a steep staircase to the cellar, where the archives were housed. She used a second key to open the cellar door and drew our attention to a small, slightly dingy powder room that had escaped my notice on my previous trip to the *Dispatch*.

The cellar hadn't changed much, if at all, since I'd last seen it. It had a high ceiling and finished walls, a tiled floor, and ample lighting, which Lilian turned on with the flick of a switch near the door. The walls were lined with utilitarian metal shelves that held cheaply bound back issues of the newspaper. A large metal desk filled most of the floor space in the center of the room. A molded plastic chair faced the aged computer that sat on the desk, and three folded folding chairs leaned against a set of shelves.

"My friend must have provided the extra chairs," said Lilian. "I rang her last night to let her know that we'd be working in the archives today."

We unfolded the extra chairs and arranged them around the desk, then hung our coats on the backs of the chairs because there was nowhere else to hang them. I noticed that Tilly was wearing a hand-knitted heathery-gray pullover Emma had made for herself before my sons were born. The sweater was too big for her, but the color was well suited to a dusty environment.

Lilian commandeered the plastic chair and cleared the desk by setting the aged computer on the floor.

"Is it broken?" Emma asked.

"I don't think so," Lilian replied. "It won't help us, though. They've digitized the past decade of the *Dispatch*, but those records won't tell us about Albert Anscombe or Cecilia Pargetter. We need to go much further back than ten years." She pulled four pens and four spiral-bound notebooks from her purse and laid them on the desk. "Before we begin, however, I'd like to propose a methodology."

"I'm glad someone has a plan," I said, hanging my shoulder bag on my chair.

"Let's hear it," said Emma.

"We'll start by looking at newspapers from 1837, the year Albert Anscombe was born," said Lilian, "and work our way forward to 1865, the year the banns were read for Albert and Cecilia."

"Do we have to go *that* far back?" Emma asked.

"We don't have to," Lilian replied, "but I think we should."

"So do I," I said. "We might find an 1837 society column that places the Pargetter family at Albert Anscombe's christening. If we do, we'll know that the two families were friendly. If they were friendly, we can assume that Cecilia Pargetter spent time at Anscombe Manor."

"And if she was a regular visitor," said Emma, "she could have found out about the priest hole from a servant or a family member, or she could have discovered it herself." She nodded. "Okay. We'll start at the beginning."

"If we divide the years within our time span by four," said Lilian, "it leaves each of us with roughly seven years' worth of newspapers. To avoid working at cross-purposes, Lori will take the first seven volumes, Tilly will take the next seven, I'll take the next, and Emma the next. We'll work simultaneously, each on our own volumes. When we finish, each of us will report our findings to the others, in order, from the earliest volumes"—she pointed at me—"to the latest." She pointed at Emma, then at the spiral notebooks. "Please feel free to take notes. Any questions? No? Good. Let us retrieve the appropriate volumes."

Lilian was clearly at home in the archives. Without a moment's hesitation, she led us to a cobwebby row of shelves in a cramped and dimly lit chamber beyond the main room. The gently decaying black leather–bound volumes that grouped the *Dispatch*'s back issues by year were much fancier than the more recently bound volumes. They were stacked neatly on their sides, with the gold numbers stamped on their spines facing outward.

"My early volumes are skinnier than your later ones," I said to Emma.

"They would be," said Tilly. "The earlier issues were printed before the government repealed the stamp and paper taxes that made printing lengthy newspapers prohibitively expensive. For the same reason, the type will be very small and the columns quite dense. Since there were fewer pages, the typesetters had to cram a lot into them."

Emma and I had become so accustomed to hearing Tilly's lectures that we didn't even look twice at her. Lilian, on the other hand, stared at her for a moment before moving on.

"You'll take an extra year, Lori, to even things out," she instructed.

I took all eight of my volumes from the shelf, but the others took only two apiece. We carried them back to the metal desk and began leafing through the old newspapers, searching for notices or news stories that would give us a better understanding of the link between the Anscombes and the Pargetters.

I was in hog heaven. I could have spent hours perusing the articles in the 1837 volume alone. Try as I might to narrow my focus, I couldn't help skimming through pieces on postal reform, the grand opening of London's Euston Station, William IV's death,

Princess Victoria's accession to the throne, and the nightmarish specter known as Spring-heeled Jack, an alarming individual with glowing red eyes and clawed hands who breathed blue and white flames while leaping improbable distances to ensnare his victims. I was bursting to tell the others about Spring-heeled Jack, but Emma was working so diligently that I kept him to myself.

Needless to say, it took me a while to strike pay dirt. I was reading a situation-wanted ad written by a governess whose areas of expertise included geography, history, painting, needlepoint, elocution, dancing, music, and modern French when I heard Emma utter a rapturous *"Yes!"* and realized that I was falling behind. I gave myself a mental shake and started over.

An hour passed, then two, the silence broken only by the rustle of turning pages and the shuffle of shoes as my companions retrieved fresh volumes from the distant, dusty shelves. Though sensational stories continued to catch my eye, I forced myself to concentrate on stories about local births, deaths, marriages, accidents, arrests, court cases, competitions, and celebrations.

At last, I found the Pargetters. Several branches of the family lived on several different farms near Skeaping village, and they seemed to announce *everything* in the newspaper. When they weren't getting married, producing offspring, or burying the dearly departed, they were winning point-to-points, growing enormous vegetables, and breeding champion rams. They were notably absent from the arrest reports, but they were involved in no fewer than seven successful lawsuits, all of which had to do with property rights. One branch of the family supplied the Skeaping harvest festivals with homemade cider, while another provided the ale.

I uttered my own rapturous *"Yes!"* when I discovered a few lines announcing the birth of a girl, Cecilia Rose Pargetter, on 17 June 1845, the second child and first daughter of George Pargetter and his wife, Anne. The announcement confirmed that Cecilia's parents did not live in Skeaping Manor. They were the Pargetters of Leyburn Farm, and Leyburn Farm was, like the other Pargetter farms, in the general vicinity of Skeaping village. I did not, however, find out if Cecilia became an accomplished horsewoman or if she cultivated gigantic turnips in later life, because my segment of the search extended no further than December 1845, when she would have been six months old.

Albert Anscombe's family, by contrast, kept their names out of the local paper. Sir Stanley and Lady Margaret Anscombe were mentioned occasionally, lumped in with other guests at various charity dos in Upper Deeping, but they didn't announce Albert's birth or any other family event in my issues of the *Dispatch*. I suspected that, as minor gentry, they preferred to place their announcements in the *Times*.

I finished combing through my bound volumes before the others finished combing through theirs. While I was rereading my notes, my stomach informed me that it was lunchtime. I was about to run out for an emergency bag of roasted chestnuts when the cellar door opened and a pudgy young man in a tweed jacket and twill trousers strode up to the desk, carrying a picnic hamper.

I recognized him immediately as Desmond Carmichael, the bespectacled journalist who'd opened the cellar door for Kit and me when we'd needed to consult the archives. Desmond greeted Lilian warmly, but a broad grin split his round, shiny face when he spotted me.

"Lori!" he exclaimed. "I didn't expect to see you here. How's the shoulder?"

"It still aches a bit in wet weather," I responded.

Tilly eyed me with concern. "I didn't realize you were injured, Lori."

"It's nothing," I assured her.

"Nothing?" Desmond snorted derisively, then turned to address Tilly. "You're in the presence of a celebrity. Lori was shot by a maniac on Erinskil Island in Scotland five years ago. The story was in the *Times*!"

"My claim to fame," I said dryly.

"You were *shot*?" Tilly said, looking horrified.

"Only once, and it healed," I said.

Tilly looked at each of us in turn, then shook her head, saying in awestruck tones, "You do lead such *interesting* lives."

"I'll try to remember that the next time I wipe Bess's nose," I said. "What's in the hamper, Desmond?"

"Tea," he replied. "Orders from on high. Mrs. Dalrymple's exact words were 'Make sure they take a tea break, Des! Lilian may be able to live on air, but her friends will be gasping for a cuppa.'"

"Antonia knows me too well," Lilian said, smiling.

Desmond passed the hamper to her. "I've supplemented the tea with gingerbread from the Christmas market."

"You're my hero," I told him.

"Mine, too," said Lilian. "Please thank Antonia for me."

"Will do, Mrs. Bunting," he said. "If there's anything else you need, please feel free to ring me."

Desmond accepted our heartfelt if somewhat bleary-eyed

thanks and left. We made room on the desk for the hamper, which was elegantly furnished with everything we needed for a tea break, including two insulated flasks of Earl Grey.

"Is Antonia the publisher?" I asked Lilian as she filled our cups.

"Antonia Dalrymple bought the *Dispatch* twenty-five years ago," Lilian replied, "and she's supported it ever since. No editorial interference, no tooting her own horn, just a steady infusion of much-needed cash from her ample reserves. She believes strongly that every community should have its own newspaper."

"She's my kind of rich person," I said with an approving nod. "She'd rather support a free press than buy designer dresses."

"She has some very nice dresses as well," Lilian said with a chuckle.

THE TEA AND THE GINGERBREAD fueled a surge to the finish line. In less than an hour, the bound volumes were back on their cobwebby shelves and we were seated at the desk, notebooks in hand, ready to give our reports. In accordance with Lilian's master plan, I went first.

"Cecilia Pargetter was born into a large and prosperous farming dynasty on June 17, 1845," I said. "Her parents owned Leyburn Farm near Skeaping village, and her numerous relatives were extremely active members of the community. Their names are all over the *Dispatch*." I glanced at my notes and continued, "My issues of the *Dispatch* told me next to nothing about the Anscombes, which leads me to believe that they were too hoity-toity to bother with a local rag. They attended charitable events in Upper Deeping, but I found no evidence to suggest that the two families ever crossed paths. I imagine the Anscombes were too full of themselves to rub elbows with farmers. Over to you, Tilly."

Tilly's report was nearly identical to mine, minus the editorial comments, and Lilian had little to add to the sum total of our knowledge. By the age of fifteen, Cecilia had six additional siblings, but she hadn't yet made a mark on her vibrant little world.

At the age of sixteen, however, everything changed. Emma's notes were lengthier than ours, because her segment of the time line began when Cecilia was old enough to enter the wider world.

"The Pargetters of Leyburn Farm were nothing if not aspirational," Emma began. "In 1861, they sent Cecilia to Miss Shuttleworth's Academy for Young Ladies in Cheltenham to learn the ins and outs of polite society. Coincidentally, Albert Anscombe received his regimental commission in 1861. I spotted his name in a list of locals who signed up to serve queen and country. It was a regular feature in my issues of the *Dispatch*."

"England was embroiled in a great many wars during the Victorian era," Lilian observed.

Before Tilly could launch into a learned dissertation on Victorian-era wars, Emma went on hastily, "Cecilia must have been an apt pupil at the academy. When she was seventeen, she took the London season by storm. She wasn't presented at court, but she was the belle of quite a few balls. It seems likely that she and Albert met at one of them, because they became engaged in May 1863."

"The banns weren't read until 1865," I said. "I wonder why they had such a long engagement?"

"It's possible that Albert's parents needed time to adjust to the idea of their son marrying a farmer's daughter," said Lilian.

"Cecilia had evidently acquired the proper social skills at the academy, but she could do nothing to change her less-than-desirable lineage."

"Perhaps the Anscombes were sizing her up," Tilly suggested. "They might have needed some reassurance that she could rise above her lowly station in life and be a credit to their family."

"Arrogant twits," I muttered.

"Whatever their intentions," said Emma, "the Anscombes invited Cecilia to stay with them at the manor on a number of occasions after her engagement." There was a note of quiet satisfaction in Emma's voice as she looked up from her notebook and said, "We've done it. We've placed her inside Anscombe Manor."

"If you can place her in India," said Lilian, "I'll pay for lunch."

"Get ready to pay," said Emma.

"You're kidding," I said, sitting bolt upright. "Can you really place Cecilia in India?"

"I can," Emma replied. "Albert joined his regiment in India in September 1864. Cecilia went to India to visit him in January 1865, accompanied by one of her aunts. She returned to England in early April and"—Emma hesitated—"and I'm sorry to say it, but she died a month later. She was only nineteen."

Tilly sighed, Lilian bowed her head, and I uttered a soft groan.

"Her parents must have been devastated," I said.

"I imagine Albert was as well," said Emma. "He sailed home for his wedding only to find that his bride-to-be was already in her grave."

"Do you know how she died?" Tilly inquired.

"The obituary mentions a distressing illness." Emma shrugged. "It could be anything from chicken pox to cholera."

"Well," said Lilian, "at least we know why the banns of marriage weren't read for a third time in St. George's."

"And we've proved that Cecilia could have given the besan ladoo recipe to the cook and set up the Hindu altar after she returned from India," said Tilly.

They were speaking with an air of finality that baffled me.

"Yes, but we still don't know who M. is," I pointed out. "We still don't know who gave the golden heart to Cecilia."

"We may never know," said Tilly. "I doubt that such a gift would be mentioned in the *Dispatch*."

"There must be another way to find out who gave it to her." I planted my elbows on the desk and leaned forward, saying urgently, "I can't prove it, but I'm convinced that Cecilia Pargetter was expressing her love for M. when she created the Hindu altar. He clearly meant a lot to her. He may have meant more to her than Albert did. Do you really want to consign the great love of her short life to oblivion? I think Cecilia would want *someone* to remember his name."

"If what you're saying is true—and it's a big if," said Emma, "how do you propose we go about identifying M.?"

"Give me a minute." I sank back in my chair and folded my arms. "I'll think of something."

I'd exceeded my self-imposed time limit by several minutes when the cellar door opened again and Desmond reappeared.

"Afternoon, all," he said amiably. "Mrs. Dalrymple asked me to ask you if the flasks need a refill."

"Thanks, Desmond," said Lilian, "but I think we've finished here."

"Did you find what you were looking for?" he inquired, but

before anyone could answer, he added, "What were you look-ing for?"

"We were gathering information about two Victorian fami-lies," Lilian told him. "The Anscombes of Anscombe Manor and the Pargetters of—"

"Skeaping," Desmond interrupted. "The Anscombes are par-venus compared to the Pargetters. The Pargetters have been around since before the Norman conquest."

"Are they still around?" I asked, warmed by the faintest flicker of hope.

"Oh, yes," he said. "George Pargetter won the wonky parsnip competition at the agricultural show in August. Tickled him pink. You'd never guess he's one of the richest landowners in the county."

"George Pargetter?" I said, peering at him incredulously. "George Pargetter of Leyburn Farm?"

"That's the chap." Desmond nodded. "There's always been a George Pargetter at Leyburn Farm, and they've always won prizes for their vegetables. If you're done, I'll take the hamper. Would you like me to lock up after you?"

"We'll take care of it," said Lilian. "And thanks again, Des-mond. The gingerbread was delicious."

Desmond departed with the hamper and I leaned forward again.

"Cecilia's father was named George," I said excitedly. "She grew up at Leyburn Farm."

"We're not going there, Lori," said Lilian, preempting my proposal.

"We have to go there," I insisted. "This is a family with a strong sense of tradition. They recycle family names. They grow news-worthy vegetables, just as their ancestors did. It's not far-fetched to assume that they hang on to family heirlooms as well. Cecilia's letters or her diaries might be stashed in an old steamer trunk in the attic"—I blinked as a brilliant thought blinded me—"possibly the *same* steamer trunk she used when she traveled to India! Can you think of a better place to look for clues about M.?"

"It's the week before Christmas," Lilian reminded me. "Now is not the time for us to introduce ourselves to the Pargetters and ask if we might rummage through their attic."

"I don't know," Emma said, pursing her lips judiciously. "Christmas can be stressful. They might welcome a distraction."

Lilian regarded her dubiously. "Don't tell me you agree with Lori."

"But I do agree with her," said Emma. "I'm not as convinced as she is that M. was Cecilia's one great love, and I'm not as confi-dent as she is about discovering M.'s identity in an old steamer trunk, but I'd rather do something than nothing. I think we should visit Leyburn Farm. If the Pargetters are too busy to see us, we'll leave."

"And come back again after the holidays," I murmured.

"What do you think, Tilly?" Lilian asked.

Tilly looked alarmed to be asked for her opinion, but she gave it with only a faint quaver in her voice. "I'm sorry, Lilian, but I'm afraid that I, too, would like to find out who M. is. We've come so far. It would be a pity to give up now."

I could sense that Lilian was wavering, so I went in for the kill. "It would give you another excuse, er, I mean, reason to avoid visiting Opal Taylor."

"All right, then," she said. "We'll go." She raised a hand to keep me from cheering. "But not today. My eyes are tired, I'm filthy, and we haven't had lunch yet. Besides, I think we should ring the Pargetters before we drop in on them."

"Do you honestly believe that they'll listen to us over the phone?" I said incredulously. "They'll take us for prank callers and hang up before we get past 'My friends and I found this priest hole. . . .'"

"You may be right about speaking to them in person," Lilian conceded. "We may *sound* deranged, but we'll *look* sincere."

"Shall I pick the three of you up tomorrow?" I asked. "Same time, same places?"

"Works for me," said Emma. "I'll do the navigating. It shouldn't be too hard to figure out where one of the richest landowners in the county lives."

"Don't forget to bring the heart," I told her. "We can use it as bait. If a fist-sized hunk of gold doesn't grab their attention, I don't know what will."

"And if the telephone rings before you arrive," said Lilian, "I'll let Teddy answer it!"

Eighteen

As a tribute to Albert and Cecilia, we had lunch at an Indian restaurant in Upper Deeping. True to her word, Lilian footed the bill. I kept my promise to myself by procuring a bag of roasted chestnuts from the market in the square before we left town. In keeping with the spirit of the season, I shared them with my companions on the way home.

It was dark by the time I walked into the cottage, but since the sun had set at four o'clock, it wasn't unreasonably late. To avoid contaminating Bill and the children with archival filth, I took a quick shower before I hugged them.

Bill had gotten dinner under way by defrosting a beef stew I'd made and frozen for just such occasions. While it heated through on the stove, I played knock-down-the-wall with Bess and listened to Rob and Will's lively account of their relatively low-key day. Kit hadn't allowed them to gallop pell-mell across the countryside on Thunder and Storm, but he had given them permission to exercise their ponies on the groomed bridle trails.

When Bess realized that her brothers were talking horses, she chimed in with "Toby! Daddy! Toby!" which, Bill explained, meant that Bess had "ridden" the good-natured pony around the indoor ring while Daddy held on to her and Nell held on to the bridle. Bess was clearly under the impression, however, that she'd won a race at Ascot.

After lunch at the tearoom, they'd taken a walk by the river, where they'd spotted a blue heron, a pair of tufted ducks, a flock of wigeons, and the entrance to a water vole's burrow. Rob had claimed victory in the stone-skipping championship with a beauty that left no fewer than seven rippling circles in its wake before it splashed down. When the sun had begun to sink toward the horizon, they'd returned to the cottage to change out of their wet wellies and to warm their cold feet before the fire.

The hearty stew put the finishing touch on a day filled with fresh air and exercise. Bess nearly dozed off during dinner, and the boys were in bed and asleep by eight o'clock. Bill was tuckered out, too, but before he went upstairs he cuddled up with me on the sofa and filled me in on a few tidbits he'd gleaned from Henry Cook at the tearoom.

"Despite being bedridden," he said, "Elspeth Binney caught a glimpse of Mr. Barlow opening the lytch-gate for Tilly Trout before they went into the church yesterday."

"Elspeth's cottage is across the lane from the churchyard," I reasoned. "The fog may have obscured the view from her bedroom window, but a glimpse is all it takes to start tongues wagging in Finch."

"They're wagging, all right," Bill said with a laugh. "Elspeth picked up the phone and shared her scoop with the rest of the Handmaidens, who shared it with every other busybody in Finch. As soon as Sally Cook heard the news, she began pestering Henry to buy a new suit for Mr. Barlow's wedding. Then Tommy Prescott showed up and she began to talk about Bree's wedding!"

Since I'd engaged in similar flights of fancy—and since I was a Finch-trained snoop—I felt compelled to defend Sally.

"It may sound silly to you," I retorted, "but I'll bet you a gallon of eggnog that Sally turns out to be right on both scores."

"I guess I'd better buy a new suit," Bill said, snickering. "How was your day at the *Dispatch?*"

"Dirty but rewarding," I replied. "I'd give you a rundown of everything we learned, but you'd doze off before I was halfway through. We're heading out again tomorrow to continue our quest. If good fortune smiles upon us, we may finish it. Will you be able to survive another day without me?"

"I'll not only survive," said Bill, "I'll flourish. Our agenda includes a tour of the miniature village in Bourton-on-the-Water."

I sighed wistfully. "Wish I was coming with you. Bourton is gorgeous at Christmas."

"I wish you could come, too," he said, "but you can't abandon your quest at this late stage. Emma would court-martial you for dereliction of duty."

"She'd put me away for life," I agreed ruefully. "She took our research so seriously that I couldn't even tell her about Spring-heeled Jack."

"Who or what is Spring-heeled Jack?" Bill asked.

"He was a Victorian bogeyman who breathed blue and white flames," I said. "He jumped out at carriages and leaped onto rooftops and terrified people with his glowing red eyes and clawed hands." I heaved another sigh. "It was *such* a juicy story."

"You can tell it to the boys on Christmas Eve," Bill suggested. "Telling spooky tales at Christmastime is a time-honored English tradition."

"Great idea," I said. "I'll tell the boys about Spring-heeled Jack, and you can deal with Peggy Taxman when they start jumping out at her."

"On second thought," Bill said quickly, "maybe we should stick with *A Christmas Carol*." He was overcome by a massive yawn. "I know it's only half past nine, love, but I'm hitting the sack."

"I'll be up soon," I told him.

"I'll be asleep," Bill mumbled through another gargantuan yawn.

After a thorough and thoroughly enjoyable good-night kiss, Bill headed upstairs and I headed for the study. Having breathed stale air and gotten next to no exercise all day, I wasn't the least bit tired.

"Hi, Reg," I said as I turned on the mantel lamps. "I promise never to take you to the *Dispatch*'s archives. You'd turn from pink to gray in about five minutes."

My pink flannel bunny seemed content to stay where he was. I paused to light a fire in the hearth, then curled up in one of the tall leather armchairs with the blue journal in my lap.

"Dimity?" I said as I opened the journal. "I've met Mr. Barlow's nephew."

Good evening, Lori. Well?

"He's a gentle giant," I said. "He must be six four and he's built like a blacksmith, but he speaks with the voice of an angel, and he smiles like one, too. He's good-looking, though his hair is way too short for my taste. I hope Bree convinces him to grow it out."

Will he allow her to convince him?

"I'm pretty sure he will," I said. "He doesn't seem to mind taking orders from her."

A most propitious sign.

"He referred to her as 'the boss' when she shouted at him," I said, "and he grinned when he told me she keeps him on his toes."

He's beginning to sound ideal.

"He's also familiar with Finch," I went on. "According to Lilian, he spent his summers here when he was a boy."

Why hasn't he visited lately?

"He joined the army when he was eighteen," I explained. "He served in Afghanistan until he lost the lower part of his left leg to a roadside bomb that killed four of his fellow soldiers. He sustained head injuries, too. Lilian reckons he spent a long time in rehab."

I hope he received the best possible care.

"He looked incredibly healthy to me," I said. "He walks with a slight limp, but if Mr. Barlow hadn't told me about his leg, I wouldn't have guessed that it was a prosthesis."

The head injuries worry me more than his missing leg, Lori. They can affect a man for the rest of his life. He may have flashbacks, nightmares, violent mood swings . . . I've seen it all before. Some of the men who came home from the Second World War never recovered from their head wounds.

"Bree is like a daughter to Mr. Barlow," I reminded her. "He wouldn't set her up with a guy who was unstable."

You're quite right. He wouldn't. I'm reassured, though I wish Tommy had returned to Finch sooner. I can think of no better place in which to recover from the visible and the invisible wounds of war. Nature's balm can work wonders, as can a sense of belonging, When the villagers find out what Tommy's endured, they'll wrap their arms around him.

"I'm kind of hoping Bree will, too," I said.

Fingers crossed! Any news about Mr. Barlow's pursuit of Tilly Trout?

"It's only a matter of time before their budding romance bursts into bloom," I said confidently. "After showing her around St. George's, he showed her around the churchyard. Then he took her out for tea and scones at Sally's tearoom, and *he insisted on paying*." I kissed my fingertips, like a chef passing judgment on a tasty dish. "It was a flawlessly executed first date."

Do you think Tilly regarded it as a date?

"I'm not sure," I said. "But she called Mr. Barlow a true gentleman and said she had a most pleasant afternoon in his company."

I wonder if she felt comfortable enough with him to chat about herself? I hate to sound like Mr. Barlow's mother, but I wouldn't mind knowing a little more about his intended's background.

"If she did open up to him, he didn't tell me," I said. "Mr. Barlow and I didn't have a proper conversation, Dimity. I had ten minutes to kill while Lilian was on the phone with Opal Taylor, so I ran over to the workshop to meet Tommy. I wasn't even thinking about Tilly."

You spent the rest of the day with her. Surely you must have asked her some leading questions.

"I intended to drag her life story out of her on the way to Upper Deeping," I said, "but Lilian, Emma, and I started talking about Tommy Prescott, and one thing led to another, and before I knew it we were filling Tilly in on Bree's life story."

It's an interesting story.

"Exactly," I said. "Tilly's not secretive, and she's certainly not standoffish. If you ask me, she simply can't imagine why we'd want to know more about her. She seems to believe that everyone else is more interesting than she is."

Which, of course, makes her quite interesting. I trust you learned more about Cecilia Pargetter than you did about Tilly Trout.

"We did," I said. "The *Dispatch* was a gold mine of information about the Pargetters. There were quite a few of them, and they wanted the world to know about everything they did." I quickly recounted Cecilia's biography, from her birth to her untimely death. "You were right about checking the obituaries, Dimity. Cecilia died before the banns of marriage between her and Albert Anscombe could be read for a third time."

How sad. She must have been very young.

"She was only nineteen," I said. "She packed an awful lot into those nineteen years, though."

She did indeed. Finishing school, a scintillating London season, a dazzling engagement, a voyage to India . . . Had she lived, she would have wielded great power.

"What kind of power?" I asked.

Albert Anscombe was only a second son, but he was the second son of a titled squire. As such, he outranked the young men Cecilia would have met had she remained on the family farm. If she'd lived long enough to marry Albert, she would have been in a position to introduce her family to her husband's social circle.

"I guess that's what Emma meant when she described Cecilia's parents as aspirational," I said thoughtfully.

They prepared their oldest daughter to enter a world they couldn't enter, and she succeeded. Her marriage would have elevated the Pargetters' social standing both within their small community and beyond.

"It's a lot of pressure to put on a teenager," I said.

Perhaps she enjoyed the pressure. Some girls do. It's a pity that the newspaper is the only record we have of Cecilia's life. The Dispatch *is an excellent source of public information, but it can tell us nothing about Cecilia's private thoughts and experiences. It can't tell us who M. was, or why he entwined his initial with hers on the golden heart. I'm afraid we've learned all we can learn about her.*

"Not so fast," I said. "There's a remote—a very remote—possibility that other records exist, records that might reveal her private thoughts and experiences."

What can you mean, my dear?

"I mean that Cecilia's descendants still live at Leyburn Farm," I said. "Her childhood home has been passed down through the generations."

I imagine the farm has changed significantly since Cecilia lived there.

"The family hasn't," I said. "The current patriarch is named George, just like Cecilia's father, and he's kept up the family tradition of growing prize-winning vegetables. It's not much to go on, but I think the current crop of Pargetters could be the kind of people who maintain a strong connection to their past."

I wouldn't rule it out.

"Cecilia must have written letters to her parents while she was in India," I said. "She probably kept a diary as well.

It's the sort of thing a nineteen-year-old would do.

"I think her family would have treasured her letters and her diary, especially since she died young," I went on. "Reading them would have been like hearing her voice again. They were too precious to throw away. Like the farm, they could have been passed down through the generations. They may still exist, Dimity."

They may, but her letters won't tell you who M. is. Cecilia wouldn't have disappointed her parents by informing them that she'd fallen in love with a young man other than Albert. The stakes were too high.

"She would have confided in her diary," I said. "It's the sort of thing a lovesick nineteen-year-old would do. Her diary might tell us who M. is."

Unless her parents read it after her death, were alarmed or embarrassed by its contents, and destroyed it to protect her reputation.

"We won't know until we ask," I said.

Do you intend to contact the Pargetters?

"We're going to Leyburn Farm tomorrow," I said. "Lilian thinks it's a bad idea to show up on their doorstep a few days before Christmas, but Emma thinks they may need a holiday stress break."

They'll probably assume that you're carol singers.

"If they want us to sing, we'll sing," I said. "After they give us our figgy pudding, we'll ask if we can look at Cecilia's diary."

It's an unusual request to make at Christmastime, but I agree with Emma. The Pargetters may welcome a diversion from cooking, cleaning, decorating, gift wrapping, and the usual holiday squabbles. They may even be flattered by your attention.

"Fingers crossed," I said.

I wish you the best of luck, my dear. You're embarking on a ridiculous enterprise, but if you're incredibly lucky—and extremely polite—you just may pull it off.

"I'll let you know what happens," I said.

I look forward to your report. Good night, my dear. Sleep well.

I bade Aunt Dimity good night, returned the blue journal to its shelf, touched a fingertip to Reginald's hand-stitched whiskers, and stood for a moment, gazing silently into the fire. I had the strangest feeling that Cecilia was nearby, urging me to bring M. out of the shadows. I closed my eyes and promised her that I would do my best.

Nineteen

Nothing delayed our departure from Finch the following morning. The sky was heavily overcast and the temperature had dropped, but there wasn't a wisp of fog in the air or a scrap of ice on the lane. Emma and Tilly were waiting for me on the graveled apron when I pulled up to the manor house, and Lilian waved to us from her front garden as we crossed the humpbacked bridge.

"Teddy's on the phone with Millicent Scroggins," Lilian informed us as she climbed into the Mercedes's backseat. "I fled before he could pass the receiver to me."

"Well done," I said.

"I'm not sure Teddy would agree with you," said Lilian.

Tilly was the only one among us wearing a skirt, but no one was wearing blue jeans. Emma and I had paired impeccable black wool coats with unexceptionable wool trousers, and Lilian wore her usual tailored tweeds. It was as if we'd agreed to dress respectably in order to make a good impression on the Pargetters. I thought it a sensible, if unspoken, agreement, as it increased our chances of being regarded as levelheaded historians rather than nosy nutcases.

"Did you bring the heart, Emma?" Lilian inquired.

"It's the bulge in my shoulder bag," Emma told her, patting the bulge.

"Before we go much farther," Lilian said as I pulled away from the vicarage, "I think we should appoint a spokeswoman. We won't do ourselves any favors if we all talk at once."

"I nominate Lori," Emma said.

"Why me?" I asked, caught off guard.

"You're the one who came up with this harebrained scheme," Emma answered, "and you're the one who persuaded me to go along with it. If anyone can get her foot in the door at Leyburn Farm, it's you."

"You do have a way with words, Lori," Lilian chimed in. "I may have jumped on the bandwagon later than Emma and Tilly, but you pulled me aboard with your tale of Cecilia's lost love. You painted such a vivid picture of the diary and the bundle of letters in the old steamer trunk that I almost believed I'd seen them."

"I dreamed about them last night," Tilly admitted.

"You persuaded me, you changed Lilian's mind, and you infiltrated Tilly's dreams," said Emma. "Decision made. You're our spokeswoman."

"I'd say it was an honor," I said glumly, "if I didn't feel as though I'm standing at the end of a plank with three swords at my back."

"You'll be fine," Emma said, laughing. "You're a great swimmer."

It was the first time I'd heard my friend laugh since the night of her party, and even though she was laughing at my expense, it was better than hearing her growl.

We were held up by traffic in Upper Deeping, but once we left the market town behind, it was smooth sailing. I knew the way to Skeaping village, and Emma had figured out how to get from there to Leyburn Farm. Memories rippled through my mind as we passed the Skeaping Manor museum. I recalled the grotesque exhibits that had delighted my sons as well as the moment I'd first laid eyes on an exquisitely wrought piece of silver and a young girl with auburn hair.

"Turn left, Lori!" Emma shouted. "Left!"

I snapped out of my reverie and turned left before Emma could seize the steering wheel. The route she'd devised took us past a vineyard that stretched from the lane to a distant shelterbelt of trees. Row upon row of gnarled vines followed the land's rolling contours, looking somewhat forlorn beneath the cloudy sky. I couldn't remember seeing any vineyards when I'd first moved to England, but in recent years I'd encountered quite a few. If the vineyard belonged to the Pargetters, I thought, they'd moved with the times.

The vineyard gave way to an apple orchard, which in turn gave way to pastures dotted with sheep and bordered by low, tangled hedgerows interwoven with wire fences. Emma was the first to spot a tasteful wooden sign elegantly carved with the words LEY-BURN FARM at the mouth of a wide, blacktopped drive. I didn't need her to prompt me to turn at the sign, but she prompted me anyway.

We crossed a rushing stream on a sturdy stone bridge and passed clusters of modern, steel-framed agricultural buildings before we began to climb gradually toward a farmhouse that crowned the crest of a modest hill. Though modest, the hill was the highest point for miles around. Since the blacktopped drive was well maintained and as straight as an arrow, I allowed myself to glance away from it every now and then to enjoy the sweeping views of the countryside.

The farmhouse was neither modern nor steel-framed. Clad in overlapping dark-brown weatherboards and topped with a sloping red-tiled roof pierced by chimneys and small dormer windows, it looked as if it had settled comfortably into the hill, like a sleepy old dog on a sofa. The central and largest section was three stories tall, with a two-story extension on one side, a one-story wing on the other, and a jumble of wooden outbuildings behind it.

The Christmas decorations would have been a touch too gaudy for my taste if assorted bicycles, skateboards, and soccer balls hadn't argued for the presence of children in the house. A miniature sleigh and eight tiny reindeer had been affixed to the highest roof at an appropriately dramatic angle, while on the ground a cordon of giant candy canes encircled a glowing, life-sized plastic Santa. A sparkly white wreath inset with blinking stars hung on the front door, and strings of multicolored lights outlined each window and every inch of the irregular roofline. I imagined the farmhouse would stand out like a cheerful beacon at night.

"More proof that the Pargetters respect tradition, Lori," Lilian observed. "They haven't torn down their lovely old farmhouse and replaced it with a contemporary monstrosity."

"They've chosen preservation over ostentation," Tilly said approvingly.

"They may be rich, but they're not show-offs," said Emma. "I like them already."

"Let's hope they like us," I said under my breath.

Smoke curling from the redbrick chimneys indicated that someone was at home, though the row of vehicles parked in front of the house also served as a fairly reliable indicator that the place wasn't deserted. I counted five sedans, two pickup trucks, and three SUVs.

"It looks as though they're having a party," said Emma. "Could be a family reunion."

"I hope it's the latter," said Lilian. "There's always at least one person who longs to escape from a family reunion."

"Do you know what you're going to say, Lori?" Emma asked.

"'Please don't set the dogs on us,'" I replied stoically. "I'll see where it goes from there." I pulled in beside an SUV and switched off the engine. "Just remember to be polite, and if they mistake us for carolers, lead with 'Deck the Halls.' The fa-la-las will put them in a good mood."

"Why should they mistake us for carolers?" Tilly asked, sounding bewildered.

"Why else would four strangers show up on their doorstep a few days before Christmas?" I retorted. "We can reveal the real reason for our visit after they invite us in for the customary cup of hot cocoa or mulled wine."

"Your mind works in mysterious ways," Emma commented, and got out of the car.

My cowardly companions arrayed themselves behind me at a discreet distance as I approached the front door. I could hear loud voices and peals of laughter coming from within the farmhouse when I reached the doorstep. After I rang the doorbell, however, all I could hear was the scrabble of claws and a cacophonous chorus of barks.

"Good grief," I muttered nervously. "I was kidding about the dogs."

"Wish I'd brought some sausages," Emma murmured.

A voice ordered the dogs to back up, and a pink-haired teen-aged girl wearing glittery reindeer antlers and an elf costume opened the door.

"Merry Christmas!" she cried, beaming at us. "Don't mind the pups. They're a bit overexcited. I promise you, they wouldn't hurt a fly."

The pups included a Rottweiler, a German shepherd, an Irish wolfhound, a Yorkshire terrier, a King Charles spaniel, and a few dachshunds, all of whom were staring at us as if we were sausages.

"What is it this time?" the girl asked with a friendly smile. "Salvation Army? Help for Heroes? Donkey Sanctuary?"

She evidently thought we were there to collect charitable donations, which at least excused us from raising our voices in song.

"None of the above," I told her, and took a bold shot in the dark. "We'd like to speak with the family historian."

"You want Auntie Rose," said the girl, as if I'd made a routine request.

From the corner of my eye I could see Emma, Lilian, and Tilly exchange surprised glances as my shot in the dark hit the target, but no one was more surprised than I was.

"Come in, won't you?" the girl continued. "I'll let Auntie Rose know you're here. *Behave, you mongrels!*"

The command was directed at the pups rather than at us, and to my relief, it was obeyed. The dogs wagged their tails and sniffed us enthusiastically after we crossed the threshold, but they didn't jump up on us, nip at our ankles, or tear our throats out. The Rottweiler took a shine to Emma, the Yorkshire terrier frisked at Tilly's heels, the King Charles spaniel licked Lilian's hand, and the Irish wolfhound gazed at me worshipfully while I scratched his handsome head.

The girl left us in a low-ceilinged, square entrance hall with a black-and-white tiled floor and a door in each of its white plaster walls. A wooden trough beside the front door was filled with mud-stained Wellington boots; coats and jackets hung from an elaborate Victorian coat tree; and scarves, stocking caps, and mittens were heaped willy-nilly on a fine Jacobean settle. The air was filled with the mingled scents of cinnamon, nutmeg, and woodsmoke.

A dozen joyously raucous children streamed past us at one point, yelling at the tops of their lungs as they emerged from the door on our right and disappeared through the door on our left. The dogs took off after them, leaving us on our own, though we could still hear the clamor of voices and laughter coming from other parts of the house.

"'Auntie Rose'?" Lilian said quietly. "You don't suppose her first name is Cecilia, do you?"

"It's a distinct possibility," I said. "The Pargetters like to recycle family names, remember."

"The girl let us in too easily," said Emma. "Why didn't she ask us any questions?"

"Your guess is as good as mine," I said, "but let's not look a gift horse in the mouth."

The door opposite the front door opened and a burly middle-aged man with a walrus mustache stepped into the hall. He was dressed in baggy corduroy trousers, a blue pullover sweater, and a Santa hat, and if he was surprised to see us, he didn't show it.

"Salvation Army?" he inquired politely.

"Auntie Rose," I replied.

"She'll be with you shortly," he informed us. "She's finishing up a game of chess. Mate in two moves, I reckon. Throw your coats on the coat tree, if you like. Wouldn't want you to over-heat." He tipped his Santa hat to us cordially and exited through the door on our left.

"Why do they keep asking if we're with the Salvation Army?" I said, unbuttoning my impeccable coat. "We're not wearing uni-forms."

"I suppose it's the first charity that springs to mind when they see four neatly dressed ladies of a certain age," said Lilian.

"I still have quite a few years to go before I reach *a certain age*," I protested, "but I do prefer 'neatly dressed' to 'dowdy.'"

We'd just managed to find hooks for our coats on the coat tree when the door on our left opened again and a striking woman walked toward us. She was tall, slender to the point of emacia-tion, and stylishly dressed in an oversized pale-pink satin blouse and flowing oyster-gray trousers. She wore her snow-white hair in a chic pixie cut, and she needed no makeup to emphasize the brilliance of her blue eyes.

"I'm told you wish to speak with the family historian," she said in a breathy but authoritative voice. "That would be me." She ex-tended a painfully thin hand to me. "Rose Pargetter Hilliard."

"Lori Shepherd," I said, gripping her hand lightly for fear of breaking it. I introduced Emma, Lilian, and Tilly, then said, "We're sorry to intrude on you and your family, Mrs. Hilliard, but we recently stumbled across a rather perplexing mystery, and you may be the only person on earth who can help us to solve it.

It involves one of your ancestors." I watched her closely as I added, "Her name was Cecilia Rose Pargetter."

"I'm afraid you'll have to be more specific," Mrs. Hilliard said with a good-natured chuckle. "I'm the fifth Cecilia Rose Pargetter in our family. The seventh opened the door to you."

"Our Cecilia was born in 1845," I said.

"The first Cecilia." Mrs. Hilliard nodded, then peered at us with polite curiosity. "Forgive me for asking, but are you associated with a university or with a historical society? I have many connections in the academic world, but I'm afraid your names don't ring any bells."

"We're not academics," Emma piped up, "but I live at Anscombe Manor."

"Good heavens," said Mrs. Hilliard, looking thunderstruck. "I don't know if I can solve your mystery, but I'd very much like to hear what you have to say about my ancestor and Anscombe Manor. Please, come through to my sitting room. It's the quietest place in the house!"

Twenty

We followed Mrs. Hilliard through the door on our right and down a long, well-lit corridor hung with colorful paper chains. While she walked, she spoke into a cell phone, asking Mary Charlotte to bring tea for five to her sitting room. I wondered if the current Mary Charlotte had also inherited her names from a forebear.

"I would have offered you tea in any case," Mrs. Hilliard explained as she slipped the phone into her trouser pocket, "but I've been playing chess with my ten-year-old grandniece and I've worked up a raging thirst. I almost regret introducing her to the game. She's fiendishly clever!"

Our hostess opened a door at the end of the corridor and ushered us into a pleasantly airy room with a broad window that overlooked the pastures, the orchard, the vineyard, and the cottages on the outskirts of Skeaping village. Framed etchings of village churches and vast cathedrals hung on the whitewashed walls, oak beams ribbed the ceiling, and a plush pale-blue carpet covered the uneven wooden floor. The carpet was strewn with toys, teddy bears, and storybooks, suggesting that Auntie Rose's sitting room wasn't always the quietest place in the farmhouse.

A diminutive walnut desk flanked by low bookcases faced the broad window. A grouping of armchairs, small tables, and a love seat sat before a log fire burning merrily in a stone hearth.

Another armchair, this one paired with a plump ottoman, sat in a corner beside a pole lamp. The lamp's peony-patterned fabric shade matched the blue-and-white upholstery on the chairs, the love seat, and the ottoman.

I recognized some of the children in the framed photographs that crowded the mantel shelf, having watched them tear through the entry hall while we waited for Mrs. Hilliard, but a pair of rosewood display cabinets, one on either side of the fireplace, held a collection of antique photographs of men, women, and children who'd died long before I was born.

"My family's past and our future," said Mrs. Hilliard, following my gaze. "I'd show you our family tree, but it would put you to sleep in seconds. There have always been quite a few of us."

"My family tree would resemble a bonsai," I said. "I'm the only child of two only children whose parents were only children."

"How peaceful it must have been in your home at Christmastime," she said as she made her way around the room to turn on the desk lamp, the pole lamp, and the lamps on the mantel shelf. "If you move my reading chair and the desk chair closer to the fire, we'll be able to sit together quite cozily. I'd shift them for you, but I'm not supposed to exert myself." She placed a hand on her chest. "A childhood skirmish with rheumatic fever left me with a dicky heart."

While we moved the chairs, Mrs. Hilliard withdrew a slim gray archival box from a drawer in the walnut desk and retrieved a small hinged leather case from one of the rosewood cabinets. She laid the box and the leather case on the love seat, then sat beside them. Lilian and I sat side by side in the armchairs on her left, and Emma took the armchair to her right. Tilly, of course, insisted on taking the desk chair. A few moments after we'd settled in, a robust, dark-haired woman arrived with the tea.

"My cousin, Mary Charlotte," said Mrs. Hilliard. "Thank you, Mary. Would you mind very much if I asked you to be mother? I need to catch my breath."

"You should know better than to play chess with Amelia Jane," Mary Charlotte scolded as she bustled about, placing cups of tea and thick slices of Christmas cake on the small tables at our elbows. "You always get overexcited."

"My excitement arises from another source entirely," said Mrs. Hilliard. She tilted her head toward Emma. "We have a visitor from Anscombe Manor."

"Do we?" said Mary Charlotte, eyeing Emma interestedly. "Try not to spring too many surprises on Rose. She might drop dead." Laughing uproariously at Emma's dismayed expression, she departed.

"Pay no attention to Mary Charlotte," said Mrs. Hilliard. "I've been at death's door for nearly eighty years, but as I've outlived my husband and most of my friends, I doubt very much that anything you say will kill me." She took a sip of tea, placed her cup and saucer on the table beside the love seat, and folded her hands in her lap. "Please tell me about the mystery that concerns my family."

I thought I'd have to play the role of spokeswoman for the rest of the day, but to my relief, Emma jumped in before I could open my mouth.

"My husband and I bought Anscombe Manor nearly twenty years ago," she said. "We thought we knew every square inch of it, but a few days ago, at our annual Christmas party . . ." Emma went on to describe the peculiar room, Tilly's recognition of it as a covert Roman Catholic chapel, and her subsequent discovery of the unusually spacious priest hole. When Tilly shrank from explaining what happened next, I took over.

I knew that I'd never be able to recapture the feeling of utter befuddlement that engulfed me when I first saw the Hindu altar, or the awe that infused my confusion as my flashlight's beam picked out each precious object in the sumptuous tableau, but I tried. I described the vibrant silk cloth, the glittering gems, the dried marigold garlands, the oil lamp, the incense burner, the voluptuous bronze statue of Parvati, and the dazzlingly decorated elephant that represented, we thought, Parvati's elephant-headed son, Ganesha, the remover of obstacles.

"There was one other precious object on the altar," I concluded, giving Emma a meaningful look, "the most magnificent and the most puzzling object of all."

Emma withdrew the golden heart from her shoulder bag and held it in the palm of her hand, where the flickering firelight could caress the sinuous filigree. Mrs. Hilliard gazed at it wordlessly, then sighed softly and shook her head.

"Please, go on," she said. "I'd like to hear the rest of your story before I present mine."

Emma placed the golden heart beside Mrs. Hilliard's teacup, reached into her bag again, and drew from it the sheet of yellowed paper containing the recipe for besan ladoo and the single handwritten line that wasn't part of the recipe: *"April 1865. Given to me by Miss Cecilia."* After handing the sheet of paper to Mrs. Hilliard, she took up the story more or less where I'd left off.

Emma told how she'd made the Indian sweet to serve at her

Christmas party, and how the line mentioning Miss Cecilia had returned to her after Tilly noticed the *C* and the *M* entwined in the filigree. She then passed the narrative baton to Lilian, who recounted her discovery of the banns of marriage in the church records at St. George's, how they'd led to our search of the archives at the *Upper Deeping Dispatch*, and how a chance comment by a *Dispatch* reporter had led us to Leyburn Farm.

"Lori thought we ought to come here because——" Lilian broke off and tossed the baton to me. "Perhaps you should explain what you thought, Lori."

"Glad to," I said, and turned to Mrs. Hilliard. "The *Dispatch* told us a lot about Cecilia, but it couldn't tell us everything. It couldn't, for example, tell us who M. was. It seemed to me that Cecilia might tell us herself, if she kept a diary and if her diary had been preserved."

Mrs. Hilliard laid the recipe next to the golden heart, then regarded each of us in turn as she said, "I'm a professional historian and I've written many books, but I've never done as much as you have with so little. You followed a trail of clues that would have been all but invisible to less discerning eyes. I hope you're proud of yourselves. You accomplished a great deal in an absurdly short space of time."

"We're rather fond of mysteries," Lilian said modestly, conveniently forgetting to mention her desire to escape nursing duties, my abject fear of incurring Emma's wrath, and our complete ignorance of Tilly's personal preferences.

"Allow me introduce you to the girl who brought you to Leyburn Farm," said Mrs. Hilliard. She picked up the leather case she'd taken from the rosewood cabinet and handed it to me. "To her family, she was known as Cissy."

The hinged leather case opened like a book. One half of the interior was lined with crimson velvet imprinted with the ghostly image of a rose in bloom. The other half held a daguerreotype portrait protected by glass held in place by a beautifully chased gold frame. The face in the portrait stood out despite the beribboned Victorian bonnet and the heavy clusters of sausage curls that threatened to overwhelm it. It was a charming face, oval shaped, with delicate features and a pair of luminous eyes that gazed back at me with the boundless confidence of youth.

"She has your eyes," I said to our hostess.

"I think it's the other way round, but no matter," Mrs. Hilliard. "Cissy's eyes run in the family."

I looked into those eyes for several minutes before I passed the daguerreotype to Lilian. Mrs. Hilliard sat in silence while each of us examined the portrait, and when Emma returned it to her, she stood it atop the recipe, as if she wished to include the girl in our conversation.

"I'm pleased to confirm your hunch about the diary," Mrs. Hilliard said, nodding at me. "Cissy was an assiduous diarist, and we've preserved all of her writings."

I felt a jolt of elation that made me want to jump to my feet and holler *"Yes!"* but concern for our hostess's dicky heart kept me silent and in my seat.

"She recorded her thoughts nearly every day," Mrs. Hilliard continued, "which is why I was troubled when I realized that the diary she kept while she was in India was missing. I knew it must exist, because she thanked her grandmother for it in a letter. It would have been wholly out of character for her to dispose of it or to leave it behind when she returned to England, so I went looking for it. I eventually found it hidden beneath a floorboard in the bedroom that had once been hers—the bedroom in which she died."

Mrs. Hilliard opened the gray archival box she'd taken from the walnut desk and withdrew from it a handsome volume bound in light-brown leather. The cover was stamped in gold with a geometric pattern that encircled an embossed, hand-colored bouquet of pink rosebuds.

"Cissy wrapped her India diary in a length of cloth before she concealed it beneath the floorboard." Mrs. Hilliard laid the diary behind the golden heart and lifted from the box a folded length of silk shot with gold thread and dyed in vibrant hues of red and yellow and green.

Lilian, Emma, Tilly, and I gasped simultaneously.

"I thought it might look familiar to you," said Mrs. Hilliard, arranging the cloth around the golden heart.

"It's identical to the altar cloth," I confirmed.

"I believe Cissy cut both pieces from a sari she brought home with her," said Mrs. Hilliard. "She described the sari in her diary."

"Why did she hide the diary?" Emma asked.

"She didn't want her parents to destroy it," Mrs. Hilliard replied.

"Why would they wish to destroy it?" asked Lilian, frowning.

"Therein lies a tragic tale." Mrs. Hilliard gave the portrait a lingering glance, then turned her head to face us as she began, "Bright, pretty, and full of life, Cissy was her family's best hope of ascending the social ladder. I hasten to point out that her marriage to Albert Anscombe would have been as advantageous to him as it would have been to her. The Anscombes needed money, and the Pargetters had it. The dutiful daughter and the dutiful son knew full well that they would help their respective families by marrying. It was a match made in a dutiful Victorian heaven."

"Sounds ghastly," I said.

"You're not a well-brought-up Victorian girl," said Mrs. Hilliard. "Cissy derived an immense amount of satisfaction from the prospect of pleasing Albert's parents as well as her own. She enjoyed her extended stays at Anscombe Manor, and the Anscombes were delighted with her. The servants approved of her, too. The cook was especially fond of her—fond enough to swap recipes with her. It was a lowly housemaid, however, who showed Cissy the priest hole. The maid had discovered it while dusting the paneled walls."

"A housemaid," Emma said under her breath as another piece of the puzzle dropped into place.

"When her parents offered to send her to India, Cissy rejoiced," Mrs. Hilliard continued. "She could scarcely wait to see her handsome fiancé strutting about in his scarlet tunic, she looked forward to meeting his friends, and she was enthralled by the notion of exploring a country that was so unlike her own. She left England in high spirits, but within a month of her arrival in India, it all went wrong."

"What happened?" I asked.

"She became desperately ill," Mrs. Hilliard replied. "And Albert, being young, carefree, and careless, neglected her. One can hardly blame him. The sparkling girl who'd charmed his fellow officers was suddenly feverish, haggard, and bedridden. He paid dutiful visits to her sickroom, but they were often cut short by more pleasurable pursuits."

"Albert had regimental duties to perform as well," Lilian pointed out. "Surely the aunt who accompanied Cissy to India would have been better equipped to nurse her niece than he was."

"She was an excellent nurse," Mrs. Hilliard acknowledged, "but though she did her best, Cissy's health continued to decline. Regimental medical officers were called in, to no avail. Finally, the chief consultant summoned a local physician who specialized in the treatment of febrile diseases. The local physician spent many hours at Cissy's bedside, monitoring her condition and giving her various medications he'd developed in his private practice. The medications helped, but they had an unfortunate, if predictable, side effect." She turned her head to look again at Cissy's portrait. "The doctor and the patient fell in love."

Lilian and I heaved sentimental sighs.

"Of course they did," said Lilian. "How could they help it?"

"They couldn't," I said. "She was his damsel in distress and he was her knight in shining armor."

"Albert had only himself to blame," Emma said severely. "He should have paid more attention to his intended."

"Albert never got the chance to blame himself," said Mrs. Hilliard, "because Cissy never told him or anyone else of her love for the doctor. Her sense of duty kept her from following her heart. She couldn't bear the thought of disappointing her family."

"In Victorian times, a doctor would have occupied a lower rank in society than the son of a titled squire," Lilian allowed.

"The doctor's social status wasn't the problem," said Mrs. Hilliard. "The problem was that he was Indian and Hindu, while she was English and Christian."

"Oh, dear," said Lilian, her face falling. "It would have been difficult, if not impossible, for them to overcome the appalling prejudices that infected so many minds at the time. I doubt that either his family or hers would have approved of their relationship. If he and Cissy had married, they could have found themselves cut adrift from everyone they held dear."

"It was the wrong period in history for them to fall in love," said Tilly.

I jumped at the sound of her voice. It had been so long since she'd spoken that I'd almost forgotten she was there.

"Before the Indian Rebellion began in 1857," she went on, "the British East India Company encouraged intermarriage as a way of promoting commercial trade. After the rebellion, there was a much stricter separation between the two communities. Those who flouted convention often paid a high price. They ran the risk of being disowned by their families, dismissed from their jobs, and harassed by their neighbors. Some were killed. The extremely wealthy could get away with it, but a doctor wouldn't have had the resources to protect himself and his wife from abuse."

"Well said," Mrs. Hilliard observed, "and quite correct. Are you a historian, Miss Trout?"

Lilian, Emma, and I chorused, "No."

"No," Tilly murmured, blushing.

"You have a better-than-average grasp of the period," Mrs. Hilliard said with an approving nod. "When Cissy's aunt saw which way the wind was blowing, she whisked her niece back to

England. Her decision was understandable, but it had tragic consequences. Cissy wasn't strong enough to endure the rigors of a lengthy sea voyage. She suffered a relapse of her illness and succumbed to it only a few weeks after she came home to Leyburn Farm." Mrs. Hilliard looked toward the broad window in front of the walnut desk. "She was buried in our section of the churchyard in Skeaping village."

"The poor child took her secret with her to the grave," Lilian said, shaking her head sadly.

"Not quite," I said. "She hid her Indian diary to keep it from being tossed on the fire. She knew her story was scandalous, but she clearly wanted someone to read it someday. She wanted someone to know about the great love of her life." I looked at Mrs. Hilliard. "She's lucky that someone was you."

"True," said Mrs. Hilliard. "Had it been her mother or her father, I doubt that I would have had the privilege of reading her words."

"She left the golden heart behind as well," Emma said quietly. "Did she write about it in her diary?"

"She did," said Mrs. Hilliard. "Toward the end of the diary, she describes the final embrace she shared with the doctor. Before they said their last good-byes, he presented the heart to her as a symbol of his undying love." She extended a tapered fingertip to trace the *M* entwined with the *C* in the glimmering filigree. "His name was Madesh Acharya."

"Madesh," I whispered.

"I looked into his history after I read Cissy's Indian diary," said Mrs. Hilliard. "Dr. Acharya lived to a ripe old age, but he never married."

"He had a heart of gold," Lilian said simply. "His love for Cissy remained untarnished, despite her death and the passage of time."

"I wonder what Albert would have thought if he'd been aware of Cissy's true feelings?" I said.

"We'll never know," said Mrs. Hilliard. "Albert Anscombe wasn't the type of chap who'd confide his innermost thoughts to a diary. And everything worked out for him in the end. He was a shadow of his former self when he left the army, but his brother's death elevated his status and his mother found another well-heeled young lady for him to marry. By all accounts, he lived happily ever after."

"Didn't you wonder what had become of golden heart?" Emma asked.

"Of course I did," Mrs. Hilliard replied. "I searched high and low for it. It never occurred to me that Cissy could have hidden it in the priest hole in Anscombe Manor. She would have had just enough time to do it, though, and to bestow the besan ladoo recipe on the cook, before her relapse. She must have thought Dr. Acharya's gift would comfort her during her long years of marriage to Albert."

"If she wanted nothing more than to be comforted," I said, "she wouldn't have created the altar. I believe she wanted something else, something impossible." I swallowed a sudden lump in my throat and went on, "Cissy was outwardly dutiful, but I don't think she ever stopped hoping that she would somehow be reunited with Madesh. That's why she offered the heart to Ganesha. She hoped the remover of obstacles would make the impossible possible."

"A dying girl's last wish." Mrs. Hilliard nodded. "It would be unbearably sad if I didn't believe that they *were* reunited. God's heart is big enough to hold people of all faiths and races. I have no doubt that Cissy was waiting for Madesh when he finally entered heaven."

No one spoke. The silence might have gone on for quite a long time if it hadn't been interrupted by a soft but determined knock on the door. Lilian rose to answer it. A little boy marched into the room, picked up a teddy bear, and marched out. Lilian smiled at him indulgently, closed the door after him, and resumed her seat.

"You must forgive my great-grandnephew," said Mrs. Hilliard. "He's rather attached to his teddy."

"I'm impressed by his good manners," I said. "At his age, my sons wouldn't have knocked."

"He's never knocked before," Mrs. Hilliard assured me. "Mary Charlotte must have coached him." She clasped her hands together. "Well. I believe we've come to the end of our stories. Thank you for bringing the golden heart with you. I'd lost hope of ever seeing it."

Emma's brow furrowed. "I'm not taking the golden heart home with me, Mrs. Hilliard. It belongs to your family, not mine."

"It belongs where Cissy left it," Mrs. Hilliard countered. "Whatever her intentions in creating the altar, I'll forever think of it as a memorial to a love that never died."

"It's a beautiful memorial," said Emma, "which is why it shouldn't be hidden away like a shameful secret in a home that was never hers. Once you've seen it, you'll understand why it should be brought into the daylight in her true home, the place where she's remembered best by those who never stopped loving her."

"Would you allow me to see it in situ?" Mrs. Hilliard asked.

"Yes, of course I will," said Emma. "You and your family will always be welcome at—" Her words were drowned out by the sound of a heart-wrenching sob.

Tilly had burst into tears.

Twenty-one

Tilly buried her face in her hands and wept inconsolably. I stared at her, too stunned to move, and Emma looked equally shocked. Lilian, who had far more experience than we did with overwrought adults, was the first to act. The vicar's wife jumped to her feet and put a comforting arm around Tilly's shaking shoulders.

"There, there," she crooned. "There, there."

The sound of her voice brought Emma and me to our senses. I crossed to pat Tilly's back, and Emma slid out of her chair to kneel before her.

"What wrong, Tilly?" Emma asked. "Did Cissy's story upset you? Is that why you're crying?"

Tilly answered with an unintelligible wail. Emma looked helplessly at Lilian and me and sat back on her heels.

Mrs. Hilliard was on her phone. "Mary Charlotte? Please see to it that we're not disturbed. No, we don't need a fresh pot of tea. Yes, of course it's cold, but . . ." She drew a calming breath, then went on authoritatively, "Please be so kind as to ensure that no one else knocks on my door, Mary Charlotte. Thank you." She slipped the phone into her pocket, retrieved a box of tissues from the desk, and thrust it beneath Tilly's bent head. "Here you go, dear. Use the whole box, if you like. There's nothing healthier than a good cry, but you must admit that you're producing a pro-digious amount of snot."

"I'm s-sorry," said Tilly, pressing a handful of tissues to her face.

"There's no need to apologize," Mrs. Hilliard said airily, plac-ing a small wastebasket within Tilly's reach. "When I cry, I turn into a snot factory."

Tilly laughed convulsively into her wad of tissues. She contin-ued to breathe in short, hiccuping gasps as she mopped her face, but her weeping subsided after she blew her nose. When Lilian returned to her armchair, Emma and I returned to ours.

I didn't know what was going on with Tilly, but Mrs. Hill-iard's offhand comments seemed to be doing her more good than our outpouring of sympathy. Aunt Dimity's words about Mr. Bar-low and Bree came back to me as I watched our hostess take charge of the situation: *Mr. Barlow is exactly the sort of company Bree needs at the moment. He won't tiptoe around her or pummel her with ques-tions about her feelings.* Mrs. Hilliard certainly didn't tiptoe.

"Would a tot of whiskey help?" she inquired of Tilly. "I re-ceived a rather splendid single malt from one of my nephews as an early Christmas present."

"Thank you, but your single malt would be wasted on me." Tilly gave her face a comprehensive wipe and dropped the well-used tissues in the wastebasket. "I'm not accustomed to drinking hard liquor."

"It's never too late to learn," Mrs. Hilliard told her, resuming her seat.

"Perhaps not," Tilly said wistfully, "but it's too late for . . . for other things."

"What things?" asked Mrs. Hilliard. "I'll concede that it may be a bit late for you to run with the bulls in Pamplona, or to drive a Formula One race car in Monte Carlo, or to swing by your toes from a trapeze, but I somehow doubt that you've ever yearned to do any of those things."

"I haven't," Tilly acknowledged. "My reach has never exceeded my grasp. My expectations were never great."

Mrs. Hilliard considered her for a moment, then said, "You're a dutiful daughter."

"I w-was," Tilly faltered, and a tear rolled down her cheek.

The door opened without warning and Mary Charlotte strode into the sitting room, carrying a tray laden with a silver tea set and a serving dish piled high with gingerbread men.

"Mary Charlotte!" Mrs. Hilliard exclaimed in tones of deep displeasure.

"You said the tea had gone cold," Mary Charlotte explained blithely, bending before each of us to allow us to refill our cups and to select a cookie. "I can't abide cold tea and I'm certain your friends can't either."

Mrs. Hilliard looked daggers at her cousin, who carried on, regardless, but I had to duck my head to hide a smile. Mary Charlotte could talk until she was blue in the face about her concern for our well-being, but she couldn't fool me. I recognized a snoop when I saw one. Unless I was very much mistaken, which I wasn't, she'd intruded on us in order to find out why she'd been asked not to intrude on us.

Mary Charlotte glanced surreptitiously at Tilly's swollen eyes and tear-streaked face, set the tray on the desk, waved aside our thanks, and left. I had no doubt whatsoever that a story about the strange little woman who'd been crying in Auntie Rose's sitting room would make the rounds of the farmhouse within the next ten minutes. By my calculations, it would reach Skeaping village before teatime.

"You'll have to come clean now," Mrs. Hilliard said to Tilly. "If you don't, I won't be able to correct the tale my dear cousin is even now concocting about you. And you will want me to correct it. I'm afraid Mary Charlotte has a somewhat lurid imagination."

"I hardly know where to begin," said Tilly.

"I'd start with the young man," Mrs. Hilliard said knowingly. "There was a young man, wasn't there?"

Tilly turned her face toward the fire.

"No," she said quietly. "There was no young man." She gave me a shy, sidelong look. "My family tree would resemble yours, Lori. I, too, am an only child of two only children. When my father was disabled by a stroke, I assumed his role as my family's chief breadwinner. When my mother fell ill as well, I became their sole caretaker." She shrugged. "There was no one else."

"How old were you when your mother's health failed?" Mrs. Hilliard inquired.

"Twenty-five," Tilly replied. "My mother and father had their savings, and I had a steady job at a bank, so we had enough money to make ends meet, but not enough to hire a full-time nurse. When I wasn't at work or at church, I was at home, taking care of my parents. I had no time to spare for a young man."

"It's a lot of weight to put on a young woman's shoulders," Mrs. Hilliard commented. "Had I been in your shoes, I would have been just a touch resentful."

"My shoes would be much too small for you," said Tilly. "It

may sound strange, but I was perfectly content to stay at home."
A faint, self-deprecating smile played about her lips. "As you may
have noticed, I'm no Cissy Pargetter. I was never pretty or outgo-
ing or socially adept. I never aspired to be the belle of any ball.
Reading has always been my preferred pastime, and my situation
in life allowed me to read as much as I pleased."

"Is that why you know so much about Tudor architecture?"
Emma asked.

"And automobile mechanics?" I said.

"And the English Reformation?" said Emma.

"And the Hindu religion?" I said.

"And the banns of marriage?" said Lilian.

"And the history of newspapers?" I said.

"And the altered relationship between colonists and the colo-
nized throughout India in the wake of the 1857 to 1858 Indian
Rebellion?" said Mrs. Hilliard.

Tilly waited for us to stop peppering her with questions, then
answered humbly, "I've always had a wide range of interests."

"A wide range of interests?" I repeated with an incredulous
laugh. "You're a walking, talking library."

"I have a retentive memory," said Tilly, "and I had a lot of time
to read. I looked after my parents for nearly thirty years."

"You have one trait in common with Cissy," said Mrs. Hilliard.
"You have a sense of duty."

"It's not a glamorous virtue," Tilly said, "but I do share it with
Cissy. Like her, I was glad to be a dutiful daughter. I took pride in
knowing that my mother and father could rely on me. My story
would be more interesting if I'd done as Cissy did, and sacrificed
my heart's desire on the altar of duty, but I did no such thing. My

heart's desire was to make my parents comfortable in their own home for as long as possible. And in that, I succeeded."

I detected no note of pride in her voice as she turned her head to gaze into the fire.

"Tilly," said Lilian, "why do you wear a mourning brooch?"

"Because I'm in mourning," Tilly replied. "My mother and father died six months ago, within a few hours of each other. I wrapped up their estate last week. It was like saying good-bye to them all over again."

"I'm so sorry," said Lilian. "You've suffered a devastating loss."

"My pastor has been a great help," said Tilly, "but I couldn't bear the thought of staying in Oxford for my first Christmas on my own. The house would have been too empty without them. I'd always wanted to see Tewkesbury Abbey, so I made a last-minute reservation, packed a bag, and . . . and you know what happened next."

"I don't," Mrs. Hilliard protested.

"I took a wrong turn during an ice storm," Tilly explained, "and I slid into a ditch at Anscombe Manor."

Mrs. Hilliard's eyebrows rose in surprise. "Are you telling me that the four of you haven't been friends forever?"

"We're old friends," I said, making a circling motion that included Emma, Lilian, and myself, "but Tilly's new to the neighborhood."

"I'll never be an old friend," Tilly said with an ominous sniff, "because I don't live in the neighborhood." She seized another handful of tissues to soak up the tears that had begun to fall again. "I've had *such* a splendid time since Mr. Barlow rescued me. I've never discovered a secret chapel before, or explored a priest hole, or held a solid gold heart in my hand. I've never had tea and crumpets with a true gentleman, or read a Victorian newspaper, or snacked on roasted chestnuts in a car. I've never seen a young man as beautiful as Tommy Prescott, or solved a mystery as sad and perplexing as Cissy's. You've made the impossible possible for me, and now it's all coming to an end and I'll go home and I won't ever see you again."

"You'll have to introduce me to Tommy Prescott one day," said Mrs. Hilliard with a suggestive leer.

"You're trying to make me laugh again," said Tilly, "but I c-can't because I haven't even gotten to the most dreadful part."

"Which is?" Mrs. Hilliard coaxed.

Tilly blew her nose, then sat motionless, staring at the floor, as if she couldn't bring herself to look anyone in the eye. "I've never had friends before, either, but since I crashed into your ditch, Emma, I've been surrounded by people who seem to care about me. I don't mind if I never solve another mystery. It's you and Lori and Lilian and M-Mr. B-Barlow I'll miss most."

I was basking in the warmth of the moment when Emma ruined it with an exasperated snort.

"What a lot of fuss about nothing," she said impatiently. "You're not being deported to Outer Mongolia, Tilly. No one's locking you in a convent. You aren't vanishing into a black hole. You live in Oxford, for pity's sake, and if you don't want to go back there, you don't have to. Haven't I told you a million times that you can stay at Anscombe Manor for as long as you like?"

Tilly looked doubtful. "You have, but——"

"Or," I interrupted, "if you'd prefer to have a place of your own in Finch, Pussywillows is available. It's a sweet little cottage.

My mother-in-law lived there before she married my father-in-law."

"There's a cottage available in Finch?" Tilly said, as if she hadn't registered my unsubtle hint about Pussywillows' hallowed place in matchmaking history.

"Take it," Mrs. Hilliard advised. "A cottage in a village filled with people who care about you is worth a hundred empty houses in Oxford."

"It's a big step," said Tilly.

"Think of it as running with the bulls in Pamplona," I suggested. "Scary, but exciting."

"And we'll be there to catch you if you fall," said Emma.

"That's what friends are for," said Lilian.

"Well . . ." A slightly stunned smile wreathed Tilly's round face. "It's never too late to learn!"

Twenty-two

Mrs. Hilliard invited us to stay for dinner, but we declined. Lilian, Emma, and I felt as if we'd already spent too much time away from home, and Tilly was anxious to take a closer look at Pussywillows. I hadn't mentioned the cottage's location, but I thought its proximity to Mr. Barlow's house might be a selling point.

Emma insisted on leaving the golden heart with Mrs. Hilliard.

"You can put it on Cissy's altar when you come to the manor," Emma told her. "Let's wait until the new year, though. The return of a Pargetter to Anscombe Manor should be a special occasion. It would be a shame to let the holidays overshadow it."

Mrs. Hilliard didn't mind waiting. She even agreed to give some thought to the idea of moving the altar from the priest hole to a place of honor in the farmhouse. I had a feeling that the furniture in the sitting room would soon undergo a radical rearrangement.

Mary Charlotte sent us off with goody bags loaded with homemade treats. We were halfway down the long, low hill when the farmhouse's Christmas lights came on, turning it into a cheerful beacon beaming goodwill to all.

We said very little on the way back to Finch, not, I suspected, because we had nothing to say, but because we had too much to think about. In days to come we would discuss and dissect every aspect of our search for the truth, but at that moment, we were content to contemplate its conclusion in silence. Lilian seemed to speak for the rest of us when she shook her head and uttered the word "extraordinary."

As we approached St. George's Church, Lilian asked me to drop her off at Opal Taylor's cottage instead of the vicarage.

"Are you sure?" I asked, grimacing at her in the rearview mirror.

"Oh, yes," she replied serenely. "I've been recalled to my sense of duty. There's nothing remotely glamorous about waiting hand and foot on a fusspot like Opal, but what a pinched and useless life we'd lead if our only goal was glamour."

"No one will ever say your life was pinched and useless," I told her.

"No one will ever say I was glamorous, either," said Lilian. She looked down at her goody bag and sighed. "I doubt that I'll salvage a single gingerbread man for Teddy. Opal has a ferocious sweet tooth."

Since Opal Taylor's cottage was across the lane from the churchyard, and since Mr. Barlow could frequently be found working in the churchyard, it came as no surprise to me when he bustled through the lytch-gate, ostensibly to say hello to all of us. I felt duty-bound to use the master control to lower Tilly's window.

"You're back late," he said.

"It's half past three," I pointed out.

"So it is," he conceded as the clock on the church tower began to chime. "I keep forgetting how quickly the light fades in December."

Lilian opened her door and the interior light came on, illuminating Tilly's face. Mr. Barlow took one look at her and frowned.

"Why're your eyes all bloodshot, Miss Trout?" he said. "You haven't been crying, have you?"

"I've been making a great nuisance of myself," she replied, "but I feel better now. Would you . . ." Her voice quavered and she paused to take a steadying breath before she started again. "Would you care to share a pot of tea with me at the tearoom, Mr. Barlow? I'm told you know every cottage in Finch inside out. I'd like to ask you about one of them."

"Right this minute?" Mr. Barlow said blankly.

Tilly looked disconcerted. "If you're busy—"

"I'm not," Mr. Barlow said hastily. "Never been less busy in my life." He opened her door, then closed it after he'd helped her to her feet. Rapping the roof, he said, "You go ahead, Lori. I'll see to it that Miss Trout gets back to the manor in one piece."

He took Tilly's goody bag from her and offered her his arm. She tucked her hand into the crook of his elbow and they walked together across the village green. Lilian, who sat half in and half out of the car, chuckled softly.

"Our little Tilly, asking a man out on a date," she said. "Whatever will she do next?"

"Marry him, I hope," I said.

"*Oh,*" said Emma, as if the scales had fallen from her eyes. "Mr. Barlow has a crush on Tilly. I've been wondering why he keeps showing up at the manor."

Lilian and I exchanged looks.

"Wow," I said.

"Sharp as a knife," said Lilian. "Well, I'd better grasp the nettle before I forget what I just said about the virtues of doing one's duty. I'll see you both at Midnight Mass, if not sooner."

"See you then," we chorused.

I took off before Opal could open her door.

Emma was lost in pensive silence until we crossed the humpbacked bridge, when she asked, "Does everyone in Finch know about Tilly and Mr. Barlow?"

"Sally Cook's been pestering Henry to buy a new suit for the wedding," I replied.

"How did I miss it?" said Emma, looking flabbergasted.

"You've been preoccupied by the Cissy saga," I said cautiously. "*Extremely* preoccupied. Preoccupied to the point of incivility. To put it bluntly, but with love, you've been as cranky as a teething baby ever since Tilly discovered the priest hole. What's going on with you, Emma?"

"If you really must know, it's the day nursery," she said. "The noise is driving me crazy."

"Nope," I said, shaking my head. "I'm not buying it. You and Derek have been renovating the manor ever since you moved into it, and I've never heard you complain about the noise. Try again."

From the corner of my eye, I saw Emma's lips tighten. For a second I thought she was going to growl at me again, but when she spoke she seemed more ashamed than angry.

"All right," she said. "It's not the noise. It's the constant reminder of what's to come."

"What's to——" I gave her a baffled glance. "Are you talking about your forthcoming grandchild?"

"I'm terrible with babies, Lori," she said.

"Nonsense," I retorted. "You were great with Will and Rob when they were little, and you've always been great with Bess."

"They don't live under my roof," she said darkly. "Nell was five and Peter was ten when I married Derek. I was relieved that I wouldn't have to change their diapers or spoon-feed them or listen to them scream at night. Derek has more maternal instinct in his little finger than I have in my entire body. I'm just not cut out to be a grandmother. Having a baby in the house will drive me mad, I know it will."

"And the Cissy mystery gave you a chance to focus on something other than the blessed event you've been secretly dreading for the past five months," I said. "Right?"

"Right," Emma said miserably. "Now that we've solved it, I don't know what I'm going to do."

"What a lot of fuss about nothing," I said, imitating the tone of voice she'd used when she'd criticized Tilly.

"Very funny," she grumbled.

"I couldn't resist," I said, "because it *is* a lot of fuss about nothing. You're suffering from stage fright, but I promise you, once the curtain goes up, you'll be fine. I've seen you nurse a colicky horse. I've seen you clean a newborn foal. I've seen you calm a fretful mare. You're a veritable font of maternal instinct, though I'd advise against using wisps of hay to clean a human baby. Too prickly."

"Ho ho," Emma said sarcastically.

"Sorry," I said, trying hard not to laugh at my own joke. I pulled onto the graveled apron at the foot of the manor's broad stone stairs and switched off the engine. "What I mean to say is, everyone has fears and doubts before a baby is born. But when you hold your grandchild in your arms, the only thing you'll worry about is whether you'll ever be able to find the words to tell her how much you love her. Or him. Or, in my case, them."

"I wish I could believe you," said Emma.

"It's true, whether you believe me or not," I said. "Besides, as a grandmother, you'll have the right to play the give-baby-back-to-mommy card. You can pull it out at any time, for any reason, but I doubt that you'll use it very often. You're going to be such an obnoxiously hands-on granny that you'll be lecturing me about the most efficient way to change a diaper."

"Sounds like something I'd do," Emma said with a grudging smile.

"I could thump you for not talking to me sooner," I said. "What's the point of having a best friend if you can't dump your worries on her?"

"Sorry," said Emma. "I'll do better next time."

"Next time?" I said, thinking instantly of Kit and Nell. "Is there an announcement you'd like to make to your best friend?"

"Not yet," she replied, "but Derek's praying for a houseful of grandchildren. If his prayers are answered, I promise to dump my worries on you *before* I get cranky."

"That," I said loftily, "is what best friends are for."

Emma grinned her old familiar grin and got out of the car. I waited until she'd let herself in through the front door, then headed for home.

I spent the evening thinking of nothing but my family. I listened to Will and Rob describe the model village in Bourton-on-the-Water, I listened to Bess describe the ducks, and I listened to Bill describe Bess's attempts to throw bread crumbs to the ducks while he kept her from throwing herself into the water. Stanley's only contribution was to purr contentedly while curled in Bill's favorite armchair.

Over dinner, we made plans to go to the Falconry Centre the following day and to have lunch at our favorite café in Moreton-on-Marsh.

"Are you coming with us, Mummy?" Will asked.

"Yes," I said firmly. "I'm sorry I haven't been around much for the past few days."

"It's okay," said Rob. "You're around now."

When the children were in bed, and I was sitting on the sofa with my head nestled against Bill's shoulder, it was his turn to listen. I told him about Leyburn Farm, Mrs. Hilliard, and Mary Charlotte. I told him about Cissy's doomed love for Madesh. I recounted Tilly's story and informed him that Pussywillows would be off the market soon, unless Mr. Barlow proposed to his lady fair before she left Oxford. Finally, I shared with him the fears that had turned Emma into a disturbingly recognizable version of me.

"Now we know why Tilly was in such a state when she crash-landed at Anscombe Manor," he said. "To lose both parents within the space of a few hours— the poor woman must have felt as if she'd lost her moorings."

"She *had* lost her moorings," I said, "but she'll find new ones. Mr. Barlow will see to that."

"We'll all see to that," said Bill. "I'm glad you talked some sense into Emma. I can't imagine why she didn't confide in you months ago."

"You don't suppose she was under the impression that I

would think less of her because I'm such a perfect mother, do you?" I said.

When we finished laughing, Bill pulled me closer.

"As for Cecilia and Madesh . . ." He shook his head. "I don't know what to say. Is it better to have loved and lost than never to have loved at all?"

"Definitely," I said. "Some people live their whole lives without knowing what it is to love and to be loved. Cissy offered the golden heart to Ganesha, hoping that he would remove the obstacles that separated her from Madesh, and Madesh never married. I think they were well aware of how lucky they were to find each other."

"I hope so," said Bill. "Do you think Mrs. Hilliard will move the altar to Leyburn Farm?"

"I do," I said. "We brought the golden heart out of the shadows. She won't want to hide it again. She'll want her family to know the true story, the whole story, of the young girl and the doctor who had their moment in the sun."

We sat in companionable silence, watching the firelight dance on the Christmas tree ornaments, until, finally, Bill stirred.

"If we're driving to the Falconry Centre tomorrow," he said, "I'd better get some shut-eye."

"I'll be up in five seconds," I told him.

"Five seconds?" he repeated dubiously.

"Maybe a minute," I said.

I jumped to my feet, ran into the study, snatched the blue journal from its shelf, and opened it while I was still standing.

"Dimity?" I said.

Good evening, my dear. Was your trip to Leyburn Farm informative?

"It was astonishingly informative," I said. "I'll tell you all about it, but not tonight. I need to spend some quality time with Bill."

Go! I'll always be here.

"Thank you, Dimity," I said, and before her graceful handwriting had faded from the page, the blue journal was back on its shelf. I gave Reginald's ears a quick twiddle, then ran back to grab my husband and pull him under the mistletoe.

No one knew better than I how lucky I'd been to find him.

Twenty-three

S ince the Nativity play had been canceled due to the Yuletide Blight's incursions on cast, crew, and audience, I spent Christmas Eve baking cookies to distribute among my neighbors after Midnight Mass. Mary Charlotte's goody bags inspired me to get out my mixing bowls, but in addition to the usual gingerbread men, angel cookies, and pinwheel cookies, I made several batches of besan ladoo. A cross-cultural goody bag wouldn't be as poignant or as lasting as a heart of gold, but it would, I thought, serve as a modest tribute to Cissy and Madesh.

A brisk east wind kept Bill and the children indoors all day, so I put them to work in the kitchen. Bess's gingerbread men were eccentric, to say the least, and I had to fend off repeated raids on my goody bags, but by the time we left for church, the cottage smelled as festive as it looked.

I felt a small pang of disappointment as we crossed the humpbacked bridge. Finch usually glittered like a gaudy tiara on Christmas Eve, but the absence of snow and the sparse decorations made it look a bit forlorn. The twinkling lights Grant and Charles had hung on their cottage were lovely, but they reminded me of the sad fact that most of my neighbors were too ill this year to hang lights on their homes.

Will and Rob were unaffected by Finch's woes. To them, Midnight Mass was a golden opportunity to stay up well past their bedtime, to belt out their favorite Christmas carols, and—if they were lucky—to catch a glimpse of old Saint Nick flying high above the village. Though a spoilsport schoolmate had broken the news about Santa's mythical status to them, and though they would have categorically denied his existence if asked, I knew why they kept their big brown eyes trained on the sky.

Predictably, Bill had to carry a sleeping Bess from the cottage to her car seat, but she was too dozy to kick up a fuss. When we arrived at St. George's, Bill and the boys went ahead to set up her travel cot while I gently extracted her from the car and carried her though the churchyard and into the church.

I thought it a pity that she couldn't appreciate the fruits of the labor she and I had put into decorating the church. The old-fashioned crèche, the red ribbons on the pews, the altar's ever-green swags, the font's Christmas roses, the sprigs of holly on the deep window embrasures, and the stout fir tree beside the pulpit had looked well enough in daylight, but by candlelight, they were magical.

In a break with tradition, we weren't the last to arrive. After settling Bess in her cot, Bill, the boys, and I made the rounds, greeting Mr. Barlow, Tilly, Emma, Derek, Peter, Cassie, Kit, Nell, Grant, Charles, Lilian, the vicar, Henry Cook, Jasper Taxman, the Hobsons, and several others, including, much to our surprise, Bill's father and stepmother. Amelia had apparently lifted the quarantine order she'd imposed on their stately home.

"My wife released me from captivity," Willis, Sr., explained, "after I threatened to sneak out of the house and walk to church to attend Midnight Mass."

"Don't blame me if you catch the wretched virus we've so far managed to evade," said Amelia.

"I have a signed affidavit stating unequivocally that I will never blame you for anything, my dear," said Willis, Sr. In a rare public display of affection, he kissed her on the cheek before adding, "I will, however, point out that our grandchildren appear to be in perfect health, and that inviting them into our home for our traditional Christmas Day brunch will not be akin to asking Typhoid Mary to tea."

"Of course you must come to Fairworth tomorrow," Amelia said to us, laughing in spite of herself. "How else will you open the gifts Father Christmas left for you?"

Will and Rob, who'd already received a pair of pocket-sized presents from their indulgent grandfather, assured her that, if Mum and Dad didn't drive them to Fairworth House on Christmas Day, they'd follow Granddad's escape plan and walk. After Willis, Sr., granted his highly intelligent grandsons permission to open their early gifts, I saw to my relief that he'd given them rectangular magnifying glasses rather than pocket knives.

When I realized that Bree Pym and Tommy Prescott were nowhere to be seen, I pulled Mr. Barlow aside to ask him where they were.

"Bree slipped on a cobble and twisted her ankle," he said. "Tommy's binding it for her. They should be along any minute now." His gaze shifted from me to Tilly, whom he'd escorted to the front pew despite her whispered protestations that she should be seated farther back.

"I see you've given Tilly a prime spot," I said. "You've been a good friend to her since she arrived at Anscombe Manor."

"I'm going to marry her," he said softly. "She doesn't know it yet, but she will."

"When did you know it?" I asked.

"First time I laid eyes on her," he answered. "There she was in her wrecked car, all shaken up and saying how sorry she was and looking like a lost puppy. She didn't know she'd found her way to me"—he smiled—"but she will. Remember when she told us straight out that she didn't think much of her name? Well, I'm fixing to give her a new one. I reckon she'll like the sound of 'Matilda Barlow.'"

"I reckon she'll love it," I told him.

I was about to squeeze his hand when the sound of Bree's voice silenced the chattering congregation.

"Put me down, you idiot!"

"Sorry, boss," said a much deeper voice. "No can do."

Every head swiveled toward the south porch as the door opened and Tommy Prescott appeared, with Bree cradled in his massive arms. Her heavily bandaged right ankle protruded from her trouser leg, and a thick wool sock covered her exposed toes.

"Sorry we're late," Tommy said to his delighted audience. "Medical emergency."

Bree buried her beet-red face in his broad shoulder as he carried her to a pew and set her down as carefully as if she'd been made of spun glass. I turned my head to see Mr. Barlow beaming at them.

"Looks like she's found the right lad," I murmured.

"There's no righter one," he said with a satisfied nod.

"Go ahead, Padre," Tommy called to the vicar as he seated himself beside Bree. "We're the last ones."

"An excellent suggestion, Tommy," the vicar called back. "If you'll all take your places?"

Those of us who were standing in the aisles shuffled into our pews, and those who were already seated picked up their hymn books. Since Selena Buxton wasn't on hand to play the organ, Lilian took her place at the fine old instrument, and with a flurry of chords that were as familiar to the congregation as the chirps of chaffinches in the spring, the service began.

I'm afraid the boys and I weren't as attentive as we should have been, but since our family always sat in the last pew, we didn't draw attention to ourselves. Between carols, Will and Rob employed their magnifying glasses to examine their hands, their clothes, Bess's cot, and the back of the pew in front of ours.

I tried to concentrate, but every time I caught sight of Tommy smiling down at Bree or Mr. Barlow sharing a hymnal with Tilly, my imagination soared. Bill had to tug on my coat to remind me to sit for the vicar's sermon.

I suspected that Lilian had told her husband the tragic tale we'd heard at Leyburn Farm, because he concluded his traditional Christmas message with a heartfelt plea to stand fast against bigotry.

"If we look upon those we meet with the eyes of the Christ child, we will see the love that binds us and reject the poison of prejudice that blinds us to God's light. We will see God's love shine forth from every face as brightly as the star that guided great kings and humble shepherds to the manger. We will love one another as God has loved us, and by so doing, we will keep faith with the babe wrapped in swaddling clothes, the child born this day in the city of David, the savior, which is Christ the Lord."

I'd seldom been prouder of my vicar. He'd spoken the words I would have spoken, if I'd had his eloquence. A true man of God, his heart was big enough to hold people of all faiths and races.

I made my feeling known to him later on, after the boys had run outside to distribute the goody bags. He credited Lilian with inspiring him, and she in turn credited Cissy and Madesh.

"How much happier they would have been had they lived at a time when differences were celebrated as gifts from God," she said.

"Let me know when that time comes," I said. "I'm afraid we still have a long way to go."

"As long as we keep moving in the right direction," said the vicar, "we'll get there."

There was a fair amount of mingling after the service, but Bree wasn't among the minglers. Tommy Prescott, declaring that he had to get ice on that ankle, carried her away before anyone had a chance to speak with her. Not that words were necessary. The look on her face when Tommy lifted her into his arms said everything that needed to be said.

The look on Mr. Barlow's face was equally expressive as he stood chatting quietly with Tilly before the stout fir tree. I didn't know what they were talking about, but as with Bree, the words didn't matter. It was clear as day that, to him, at that moment, no one existed but the shy little middle-aged woman who'd captured his heart.

"There's too much romance in the air," I said to Bill. "We'd better leave before I swoon."

I picked up Bess and Bill grabbed her travel cot. We were working our way toward the south porch when Will and Rob barreled into the church, shouting excitedly.

"Mum! Dad! Come and see!"

I could almost feel a frisson go through everyone who'd been at Emma's party. The sense of déjà vu was uncanny.

"If there's been another ice storm," Bill muttered, "our sons are going to be known henceforth as the harbingers of doom."

The cries that came to us from the churchyard sounded oddly joyful, however, and when we stepped outside, we found out why. A light dusting of snow had turned my forlorn village into a winter wonderland.

"Merry Christmas, love," said Bill.

Bess didn't stir as he bent his head to kiss me, and she continued to sleep in heavenly peace as we set out to savor the beauty of the silent, holy night.

Epilogue

pril was a momentous month in Finch. On the sixth, Cassie Harris gave birth to a healthy baby boy, who was christened Peter Derek after his father and his grandfather. Within a heartbeat of making his acquaintance, Emma discovered that she was cut out to be a grandmother. Her lectures on how to refine my diaper-changing techniques began a few days later.

Happily, those who'd been afflicted by the Yuletide Blight had recovered fully, and those who'd left the village before the blight had struck had returned. A full complement of villagers transformed Peter Derek's christening into a scintillating social occasion and inundated his proud parents with gifts ranging from an exquisite baby quilt to a sturdy all-terrain stroller.

In the meantime, the vicar read the banns of marriage for William Thomas Barlow and Matilda Susan Trout aloud in St. George's; Bree Pym surprised no one by announcing her engagement to Tommy Prescott; and Bill's tailor measured him for a new suit.

Mrs. Hilliard and a dozen other Pargetters descended on Anscombe Manor in mid-April. Emma, Lilian, Tilly, and I feted them with a luncheon that included several Indian dishes, then stood by solemnly while they took turns entering the priest hole to view Cissy's Hindu altar in situ.

After experiencing the cold, the haunting darkness, and the pitiful isolation of Cissy's hiding place, Mrs. Hilliard agreed to move the altar to Leyburn Farm, where it would be cherished as a poignant family heirloom. Before she left, she expressed her family's gratitude to us by presenting each of us with a small replica of the golden heart. I placed mine on the mantel shelf in the study.

My gaze came to rest on it one evening in late April as I sat in a tall leather armchair before the hearth, with my stockinged feet propped on the ottoman and the blue journal open in my lap.

"Cissy took us on quite a journey," I said. "From a priest hole in a Tudor chapel to a Victorian army compound in India to the farm where she was born and where she died. It's a hundred years too late, but I'm glad the Pargetters are finally celebrating her love for Madesh."

So am I. I'm also proud of you for making the celebration possible.

"Me?" I said. "I didn't do anything. Tilly discovered the priest hole. Emma had the recipe. Lilian dug up the banns, and it was her idea to search the *Dispatch*'s archives. The only items I found there were Cissy's birth date and a fantastic piece about a Victorian bogeyman called Spring-heeled Jack."

What did Spring-heeled Jack have to do with Cissy?

"Absolutely nothing," I said. "See? My only contribution to solving the Cissy mystery, if you can call it a contribution, was to insist that we go to Leyburn Farm."

I disagree. Without you, Tilly wouldn't have discovered the priest hole, Emma's recipe would have meant nothing, Lilian wouldn't have looked for the banns, and none of you would have had a reason to search the Dispatch*'s archives or to go to Leyburn Farm. Credit where credit is due, Lori.*

"But I'm not due any credit," I protested.

Of course you are. You were responsible for the ice storm that brought Tilly to Anscombe Manor in the first place. Bill is quite right, my dear. You have a gift for attracting dreadful weather.

"Bill was joking!" I exclaimed.

So am I, Lori. If rotten weather followed you around, Peter Derek's christening wouldn't have taken place on a perfectly lovely spring day. Which is not to say that you contributed nothing to bringing Cissy and Madesh out of the shadows.

"I didn't contribute anything of value," I said.

You supported your friends, Lori. You were patient with Emma, you encouraged Tilly, and you sympathized with Lilian's wish to take a much-needed break from her duties. The golden heart on the mantel may remind you of Cissy and Madesh, my dear, but it will always remind me that you have a heart of gold.

Miss Cecilia's Besan Ladoo

Ingredients

2 cups chickpea flour
1 cup clarified butter
1 cup white sugar
2 teaspoons finely chopped pistachios
1 teaspoon finely chopped cashews

Directions

1. In a saucepan over medium heat, stir the chickpea flour and the clarified butter together until the mixture smells toasty, about 10 minutes. Set aside until cool enough to handle.
2. When the flour-and-butter mixture has cooled, stir in the sugar, pistachios, and cashews until evenly mixed.
3. Form the mixture into small balls the size of walnuts. Use some pressure when shaping the balls to keep them from falling apart.